About the Author

Peter, who works with children with autism during the week and is a non-stipendiary priest in the Church in Wales at weekends, lives with his wife, two dogs, a glorious rescue cat, some chickens and six very elderly sheep in the beautiful mountains of Mid Wales. They have three adopted children and eight grandchildren and enjoy conserving wildlife in such a lovely place. Peter has always been fascinated by Anglo-Saxon legends and language, inspired by the stories of J. R. R. Tolkien when he was young.

Folcespel

Peter Ward

Folcespel

Olympia Publishers
London

www.olympiapublishers.com
OLYMPIA PAPERBACK EDITION

A CIP catalogue record for this title is
available from the British Library.

ISBN: 978-1-78830-499-3

This is a work of fiction.
Names, characters, places and incidents originate from the writer's
imagination. Any resemblance to actual persons, living or dead, is
purely coincidental.

First Published in 2020

Olympia Publishers
Tallis House
2 Tallis Street
London
EC4Y 0AB
Printed in Great Britain

Dedication

To my old friend Tony, who first introduced me to *The Hobbit*.

Acknowledgements

I would like to thank my wife, Sandra, for her outstanding patience, forbearance and encouragement, and without whom this book might never have emerged from the dark!

Introduction

'There's something rotten in the state of Denmark', my mother would say when I was young, meaning that she 'smelled a rat'. I thought it a bit odd that the rot, whatever it was, should waft from Denmark, when we lived in England, and only later found out the source of the quotation. Later still, I discovered that Shakespeare's story of Hamlet was in fact based on a tale written down by the twelfth century Danish historian known as Saxo Grammaticus. It relates to events in Jutland around 350 AD, about a century before the matter of this book, and the *Adventus Saxonum,* when tradition suggests that the Anglo-Saxons first came to British shores in the persons of Hengest and Horsa, whose alleged landing place I knew of, because my father had taken me to Pegwell Bay as a boy and shown it to me.

I started reading the works of J. R. R. Tolkien as a teenager, and have enjoyed them ever since, but only quite recently did I discover Alan Bliss's edition of the work Tolkien had done on the story of Hengest[i]. The story falls into the time we have come to call the 'Dark Ages', and indeed the lack of any contemporary written record leaves us with only glimmers in the dark of stories and people from that time, as reflected in lays and folk stories preserved and handed down (and possibly distorted!) through the generations to be set down in writing much later, often centuries after living memory of their words and deeds had perished. As a child, my father encouraged me to read the stories of ancient Greece and Rome: I could find no equivalent for the ancient tales of England, and indeed in his time Tolkien expressed a wish to amend the absence of a 'mythology for England'. In this book I have attempted to draw out a thread of history, legend or myth that relates particularly to the figure of Hengest, and also the identity of the folk whom the early eighth century historian Bede[ii] states were the original Germanic settlers of Kent, the ancient Jutes. By attempting to stitch together some of the various scraps of literature that we do have by patching in the gaps, I hope that I have not stretched the bounds of credibility too far.

The question of how the Jutes came to Kent has puzzled historians for some time. The appearance of Hengest and the Jutes in the epic poem *Beowulf*[iii] and the short fragment of a lay known as *The Finnesburh Fragment*[iv] place both man and people in Frisia, (in the Netherlands) around the middle of the fifth century. But there is an ambiguity within these poems: Hengest appears to be both an enemy of the Jutes, and yet also a leader of them. Tolkien proposed a resolution to this confusion with his theory that there were in fact Jutes on both sides of the conflict[v]: those who had sought to escape an oppressive dominance by the Angles by settling in Frisia under Finn Folcwalding, and those who had remained in Jutland, some of whom had followed Hengest to the court of Hnæf Hocing, the Danish prince or king.

In this tale I have also hijacked some other pieces for my purposes: parts of that early catalogue of the many tribes and peoples, *Widsith*[vi], as well as *The Wife's Lament*[vii] and *The Husband's Message*[viii].

It is, I think, generally accepted that the Hengest of *Beowulf* and Hengest of Kent are one and the same man: the name is thought sufficiently unusual[ix] to make it unlikely to belong to two separate individuals living at the same time in history. This story attempts to trace Hengest's path, and that of his people, from their roots in the Jutland peninsula to the shores of Britain; and in doing so, suggests that the story of Shakespeare's Prince of Denmark may have been deeply connected with the formation of England.

Prelude

435 AD

The ship shuddered beneath her as another wave broke against the side and sent a plume of spray to slap her in the face, again. Gerta was getting used to the constant rolling motion now, but felt empty and drained, having been seasick since her family had embarked on the trader the morning of the previous day. She was still confused and disorientated, not knowing quite why they had left their home, the only home she knew, so suddenly. She sat with her back to the side of the ship, where she could see most: her brother, father and uncle amongst the oars, working their passage; her mother, sitting mending under the meagre canopy that covered the bow; and most importantly, where the next wave was coming from. But the sea was slightly calmer now, the yawing of the ship less dreadful, and the spray had washed away much of the pervading smell of sick. She began to feel better, although she still couldn't face the skin of water her mother proffered her. As the day drew towards its end and the sea abated, she drew the woollen cover about her and settled on the deck, but tired though she was, sleep seemed far distant. She reached out an arm to run a finger along the edge of the dark timber planks of the ship's side. Earlier she had noticed that you could see daylight through some of the joints, and they seemed perilously thin: in this tub, you were never more than an inch away from drowning, she thought, as she wedged herself into the corner of one of the ribs, up against the pile of belongings they had brought with them after their hurried departure. She pulled out the shield, covering herself with it, one more barrier against the perpetual spray.

The shield was a family heirloom, made for a hall's wall rather than a warrior's arm, and it was marvellously decorated. A gilded boss at its centre was surrounded by radiating segments, each containing an exquisite picture of an episode from the life of her father's grandfather Amleth, last King of the Jutes. She and her brother would take it in turns to choose a picture from the shield, and their uncle, Guthere, would tell them a tale that lay behind it. She had her favourites, and some she enjoyed less. She loved how as a young man, Amleth managed to hoodwink his elders by playing the fool, disguising his wits behind a facade of absurd behaviour, such as his ridiculous trick of mounting a horse backwards; and then how the traps and snares that were laid for him all fell apart as he saw through them, and cleverly countered them. She was less fond of the one about the eavesdropper who was run through by Amleth in his hiding place beneath the straw, and his body cut up and fed to the hogs; and Amleth's clever and bloody revenge on his wicked uncle: stories her brother always seemed to choose when his turn came. As she recalled another of her favourites, the story of how Amleth managed, with the aid of his foster-brother and a gadfly, to elude his uncle's spies and make off with a girl to a distant and impenetrable fen, Gerta drifted off into an exhausted sleep.

She was awoken by the menfolk returning from their spell at the oars. Gerta's mother was doling out some bread and hard cheese from a sack. She offered Gerta a chunk of bread. Gerta eyed it uncomfortably, not yet trusting her belly.

"Come, Gerta, you must drink," said her mother, and she reluctantly accepted the skin of water and took an experimental sip. It stayed down, and she drank some more, then sat back against the ship's side. Her brother stepped over a bench and flopped down on the deck beside her. She passed him the waterskin. He was her elder by two winters, and proud of his time at the oars.

"We'll make an oarsman of you yet," said his uncle as he lowered himself to the deck with his food. Her uncle Guthere was older than his brother, his hair and beard shot with grey. Guthulf, the children's father, stood looking out to sea while he ate, his thoughts evidently elsewhere.

"Are we nearly there, uncle?" Gerta asked.

"Not that far now, girl," he replied. "Another day's pull should bring us within sight of the Frisian shore."

"Can I help with the rowing?" she asked. Next to her Garulf spluttered on his bread as he stifled a laugh.

"Fat lot of good you'd be," he smirked. "Rowing is for men, not sickly girls." Gerta scowled.

"I thought manners made a man," she muttered. Garulf ignored her.

"Tell us a story, uncle," said Garulf.

"When I've finished eating," her uncle replied, as their mother handed out an apple each from the sack.

"Gerta thinks it's her turn to choose, because she was sick," said Garulf, "but I'm sure she had her turn before we got on the boat."

"Well," said Guthere, "I'm going to have a turn, because this story isn't on the shield — it's what happened to Amleth after the shield was made."

Guthere finished his apple unhurriedly, while the children fidgeted and thumped at one another. Eventually he tossed the core over the side and settled himself on the deck.

"Listen! You have heard that Amleth, your father's grandfather, was made king by the people of the Jutes, having heroically freed their land from the fraudulent rule of his uncle, Feng, who had killed Amleth's father and usurped the kingdom, ruling our people unjustly. After this, Amleth sailed again to the land of the Britons and his wife. When he returned, laden with great treasures, and now two wives, he found that all was not well. During his absence, Amleth found that Wihtlæg, king of the Angles, had been harassing Garutha, his mother and your namesake, Gerta, claiming that her son's claim to the kingdom was illegitimate, as the appointment of kings of the Jutes was forbidden without the approval of their Angle overlord, Wihtlæg.

"Now this King Wihtlæg, despite Amleth's attempts to pacify him with the choicest gifts from his treasures, persisted in his arrogance, and gathered all the forces of his own people, together with those of their subject islands, to make war on us and our king. King Amleth's sense of honour left him no choice but to fight, but the forces ranged against him were too powerful, and he died in combat with the Angle king.

"Since that time, the land of the Jutes has been governed by the Angles. There has been peace, but we have not forgotten a time when we had our own king, and governed ourselves, and many of us look forward to a time when we will do so again."

"Uncle," asked Gerta. "Then why are we sailing away from our home?"

"Well," Guthere replied, with some hesitation, and a glance at his brother Guthulf, who continued his survey of the horizon, "...some of us think that the time has come to throw off the yoke of Anglian domination. We went around our land, urging our people to think about their freedom. Many of them were content to remain as they were, but many listened to us. Then the Angles got to hear about our activity, and it became unsafe for us to stay. As your father and I, and of course yourself, Garulf, are heirs of Amleth, they saw that we might become a rallying point for such an insurrection. But we go to a safe place. The King of the Frisians, Finn Folcwalding, has always been friendly and welcoming toward our people. He will protect us. You will be safe there, until we can return home as heroes! Now, get some sleep."

"Thank you, Uncle," said Garulf, as Guthere heaved himself to his feet. Garulf and Gerta found what wrappings and comfort they could, and burrowed down into the corners made by the ribs of the ship.

But Gerta, having slept already, could not easily sleep again. She fidgeted and turned, and eventually got comfortable enough, but the motion of the boat was still uncertain. As she lay there she listened to the subdued conversation of her mother, father and uncle. Her father was speaking:

"Why do you have to fill their heads with this nonsense? Is it not enough that your stirring up of the people has made us exiles, having lived in peace for so long, that you must excite these illusions of greatness in them too?"

"These are no illusions," his brother hissed. "If you will not acknowledge your birthright, then maybe the boy will, and find the destiny that you evidently lack the nerve to seek..." Gerta heard a scuffle, and opened a cautious eye to see her mother separating the two men.

"Enough!" she hissed, "that poor girl has suffered ever since we left, and now she sleeps. I will not have her awoken." Guthulf's hands fell from his brother's tunic, and Guthere turned away to clamber through the benches, seeking other company.

Gerta awoke as the spray once again cooled her cheek. It was a fine morning, the sun having already risen over the stern end of the ship, and a fresh breeze swept across the sea, white horses cresting the waves. The men were off at the oars again. Gerta stretched. She felt better. She got up and walked, still slightly unsteadily, but learning to ride with the motion, to the windward side of the ship. She leaned over the gunwale, facing the wind and the spray, starting to enjoy the delights of being at sea. As the ship moved into the lee of another of the islands, the motion became easier, and she dared herself to stand without clinging on to the side.

As the day wore on, clouds started to drift in from the north west, and the wind increased. The master steered a course slightly closer to the mainland shore, and Gerta could make out the line of sand dunes above the beaches, some of them lofty and green. Without warning, there was a rending groan and thump as the ship lurched and stopped dead, sending oarsmen tumbling backwards from their benches, throwing the whole ship into confusion, and leaving it heeled over to the windward side, facing the waves, which were already washing into the middle of the ship. The master sprinted across the leeward benches, shouting for axes, and leaning over to see what had struck. Gerta suddenly felt the wash of water around her ankles, and there was a grinding creak and crash as the ship settled and a huge spike of timber from the wreck they had fouled pierced the bottom of the ship, heaving up the deck like the vast upturned claw of some sea monster and bringing with it a fountain of water. With panic rising, she glimpsed her father leaping over the benches towards the stern with an axe to help cut free the handful of slaves from their oars. Swimmers were already jumping over the side, and making for the distant shore, but Gerta had never learned to swim. She turned to see her mother searching for something.

"Mamma, I'm scared!"

Her mother found what she sought — the empty waterskin, which she blew up and stoppered, then quickly lashed it tight to the strap of the shield. She hugged her daughter, then put the shield in her arms.

"Listen, Gerta. You must be brave and strong. You must hold on to this and not let go. You must kick and kick until you reach the shore."

"Mamma, I can't swim!"

"You can do anything. Now go. I love you." And with that she hoisted her daughter over the side and lowered her into the swirling current, and let go.

*

As the sun arose, two horsemen cantered along the Frisian strand. They had encountered in the first light of dawn much detritus and larger pieces of wreckage, some survivors and not a few bodies, washed ashore from the wrecked trader. The coastguard reined in his mount.

"I think we have found all that we will. Best get back to the fire and sort out the living."

"Sir! I think I see something yonder. Near the waterline."

They trotted down towards the dark object in the sand. As they drew closer, the mate said:

"Maybe not. Just a shield."

But the coastguard dismounted.

"But what a shield! And unless I'm much mistaken, this pretty shell hides a cockle within!" He picked up the shield from the sand, revealing the body of a little girl of about seven winters. He lifted a cold hand, and searched for breath.

"She's quick and breathes!" He gently lifted her, wrapped her in his cloak and set her on his mount, throwing the shield to his mate, and they set off back along the strand towards the fire.

Winterspel

Winter Story

450 AD

On an early evening in the last month, with the shoreline to our south and a wind bearing rain and stinging hail from across the sea, we rowed towards the watchman's fire on the Frisian strand. Our voyage had been uneventful apart from a broken oar when we were navigating the tricky currents round the islands; at times tedious in the headwinds; but I felt a sense of excitement, mixed with a little trepidation, for we were to celebrate the feast of Yule as guests of the renowned king of the Frisians, Finn Folcwalding.

Hnæf, our lord (and now Finn's brother by marriage to Hildeburh), Danish prince of the house of Hælfdene, stood and made his way over the men and benches to take up his position in the bow to hail the shore, as a handful of figures emerged from the dunes onto the strand ahead of us. In the middle of the ship, as the murmurs of our impending arrival spread, Sigeferth, Ordlaf and a couple of the Jutes of the resting watch looked up from their dice. Frithuwulf, Hnæf's sister-son, still a stripling, stood up from his oar, turning to view the land of his birth. And Hengest, at the steering oar, stared thoughtfully at the shoreline, but the content of his thought remained a mystery, as usual. Long of face, limb and body, dark hair flapping across his face in the wind, he set our little ship on a course to run up the strand, and a glance from those piercing eyes dropped Frithuwulf, blushing, to his bench to take his part in the last pull for the shore.

Our visit was not unexpected. After the usual exchange of formalities with the coastguard, whose eyes were flickering from one to another of us as he attempted to size up our various origins, he rode off to announce our arrival to his master, while his men joined ours in the safe berthing of the ships and we set to unloading whatever gear we weren't already wearing, with some gifts for our host. His report will have been an interesting one, for we were something of a motley crew: All Hnæf's men, but a good half of them were certainly not Danes. Apart from the various *wreccas* (freelance warriors who followed Hnæf), Hengest had brought with him his own following of Angles and Jutes, myself amongst them, who had sworn our allegiance to Hnæf at the Danish court.

As the light was failing, we marched, still on our sea-legs, out of the dunes onto firmer ground, and caught our first glimpse of Finnesburg, home of the powerful Frisian king. The burg itself was slightly raised from the saltings on a slight eminence just above the level of the tides. Its stockade seemed to run on and on into the middle distance, enclosing a settlement as vast as any I had seen. Many buildings were there within, below the magnificent high hall: lesser halls, low houses and shelters for beasts. Beyond the burg, we could just make out in the gathering darkness a hinterland gently rising, dotted with the specks of light that suggested small farms and hamlets among patches of woodland and heath. To the south lay the broad estuary of a river, the nearer shores of which were dotted with clusters of buildings that must have been shipwrights' yards and fishing settlements.

Under a gate tower of huge timbers, we were escorted through the burg. Most folk were about the business of bedding all down for a wet and chilly night, but some came out to watch us pass, mostly women and some children. Their chatter was bright and almost musical to those who had only heard the murmurs of men for days, and their speech, though accented, was easy enough for us to understand. As we reached the top of the slope, the way broadened out into the courtyard before the great hall, and beneath its wondrously carved gables our line came to a halt, as Hnæf met the challenge of the guards at the doors, and we prepared to surrender our weapons to their keeping: never a comfortable thing!

As I awaited in the line for my turn, the doors were opened, and warm light emerged from within: the smells of roasting meat, and the promise of shelter from the wind and rain of our sea passage awakened an appetite that suddenly cut through the apprehension of being weaponless among strangers, far from home: and after all, there were some sixty of us, all told, and most of us pretty handy, armed or no, if things did turn sour.

As we processed into the hall, silence fell along the benches and tables that lined each side. The roof, like a vast upturned ship, receded away into the shadows. We filed up as far as the huge firepit in the centre of the floor, and came to a halt as Hnæf stood still before the king, who was seated on a low dais at the head of the hall.

"Renowned king, Finn son of Folcwald, Sister-husband, I come in peace at this Yuletide, as kindly invited, to share this time of joy with you and yours at your table. Wonderful it is at last to look upon your magnificent kingdom!"

Finn stood up, and replied:

"You are most welcome, Hnæf Hocing, to our court. And your retinue also: do I see one amongst you has a familiar look? I believe I do, though he be much changed!"

Hnæf drew to one side, as Frithuwulf dropped to his knee before the dais.

"My son, you too are most welcome here! Get up, and come and embrace your father now!"

And from her seat at the side of the dais came Hildeburh to join her husband in the welcome. I had not seen her for many years, not since she walked with her father Hoc to the ship that was to bear her away to her husband and new home in Frisia. Hardly more than a girl then, her duty had lined her face now, but not hidden her beauty, as she embraced her son, unseen for ten years. Frithuwulf, slightly overwhelmed by all the attention, and for a moment hesitant about which way to go, returned to his place behind his uncle, staring fixedly at his feet. Finn, signalling to his serving men and women at the sides, said:

"And now you must be weary from your long and arduous journey. Sit and eat, and we may catch up with words later."

The huge hall had seemed quite full of men when we first entered, but now space was made for us at the benches. Beer was already circulating as Hildeburh moved from table to table with the welcoming cup. Hnæf, his mouth full of meat, stood and beckoned me over.

"Come, Æschere and wait on me; I need to speak words with our host."

Standing behind our lord as he sat next to Finn at the high table, I had an opportunity to scan the length of the hall while Hnæf and Finn exchanged pleasantries and news. Tables and benches ran down either side lined with warriors, serving men and women moving between them. Finn's men were of assorted shape and size, some short and broad as linden shields, some as tall as myself, that is, uncommonly tall. Finn himself was both broad and far from short, a big man in every sense; a shock of grey hair matched the beard that framed his features. Also tall, and straight as a willow wand, there stood next to me, awaiting Hildeburh's return to her place, her serving woman. Without wishing to stare, I sensed that she was very fair of face and hair, and that her features had little in common with some of the Frisian women who moved around the tables. In fact, those high cheekbones reminded me of my own mother as much as any.

My privilege as Hnæf's servant was to eavesdrop on our masters' conversation. The formalities were now over, as drink warmed the spirits, and yet something was troubling their talk.

"I cannot help but notice," said Finn in a discreet tone, "that you bring a number of Jutish men in your company."

"Aye," Hnæf replied, "and each of them a fine warrior. Hengest, my captain, brought them to my court some years ago, and I have had no cause to regret receiving their allegiance. But forgive me, my lord King, for if I am not mistaken, you also have no fewer of them in your own court."

"Indeed I do. Most of those you see were born here: their fathers and grandfathers arrived here claiming to seek refuge from oppression in their homeland. Their story was credible, and my father, Folcwald, true to his name, saw no reason to turn away such sturdy men, and welcomed them and their families, and many have since married into my own people's families. One of their number, in fact, claims descent from their last king. You see the young man at the second table, with the warrior standing behind him? Garulf is his name. He has quite a following himself."

The woman to my left stirred slightly, and cast a glance at the king, but was suddenly called away to attend to her mistress. Finn continued:

"Now, your captain, Hengest did you say?"

Hnæf pointed him out.

"'*Stallion*' is something of an immodest name to walk under, is it not?"

"Ha! Not a name he gave himself," Hnæf replied, "but one he cannot seem to shake off. There are few men that I would rather have next to me in a tight place."

Hildeburh's servant had returned to her place, and was, I think, listening as much as I to the conversation.

"Now, brother," resumed Finn, "we may have a problem. When my men of the Jutes came here from over sea and land, they brought with them songs of a people divided between some who sought to remain, and others who chose to leave and seek their fortune with other masters, far distant from their oppressors. The parting was not a friendly one — you are aware of this?"

"I have heard such songs, but thought that they belonged to a past age."

"Ah! This may be true... but there is always some old wolf who once sat on his grandfather's knee and drank in the

27

old tales. And now, after many lives of men, in my own hall, I find both parties thrown back together again. It seems well at the moment, but I deem it may not take long before the truth seeps out. I think it best that after we have eaten, I withdraw from the hall with my retinue, leaving you and your men to rest quiet here. You must be in need of it."

Finn's prophecy came to pass only too soon. There was a disturbance at the third table. Someone had, I think, chosen to make fun of the name Hengest — suggesting, I suppose, that it was not a name fit for a man. Hengest remained still, in his seat, surveying his antagonist over his ale. The other, a Frisian Jute, had risen from his bench, and leaning forward on the table said:

"Come then, what is your true name... or do you have reason to conceal it?"

"I am unashamed of my name," Hengest replied, "I am named Octa, son of Wihtgils."

The King had risen from his seat and was striding towards the table, but it was too late. A greybeard from the next table had turned at hearing those names.

"Bid him continue with his lineage," he said to the man standing, "and see if he still be unashamed."

"Sirs," interrupted the king, "such questioning of a guest is unseemly, and you threaten the peace of my hall. You will desist."

But the unanswered question hung there as the king called for music.

"Not that one!" Finn snapped, as the *scop* opened with the first notes of a particularly undiplomatic tale from Jutish history, "choose another."

But it soon became obvious that the song was not working. As I watched, whispers spread around the hall. The young man Garulf stood, and strode up before Finn's table.

"My lord King," he said, in a voice loud enough to be heard by most. "I beg your leave. I find that I cannot endure this present company."

"But Garulf, my friend, these are our guests," Finn responded mildly. "We must not insult them so."

Leaning closer to Finn's ear, Garulf hissed:

"Must we not? That one," jerking his thumb towards where Hengest sat, "is Anglekin — not only that, but Guthere there reckons him to be of the line of Wihtlæg, the ruler of Angeln who killed our king and humiliated our people. And there are others…" — his eyes glanced up at me — "men of my own blood who have betrayed their country and trail around after these wretches! I beg you, grant me leave!"

"Go, then, with my leave, as you must, and take those who follow you, for we vacate the hall for my wife's brother this night."

Bowing to the king, Garulf turned, and many men arose to follow him from the hall. Finn bowed his head. Turning to Hnæf, he said:

"I fear we have inadvertently awoken ancient mischief. I, too, will take my leave, and bid you a quiet night. You will reclaim your weapons when I have returned to my lodging. Fare well."

As the king of the Frisians withdrew with his remaining court, and the servants finished clearing away, Hnæf sent for our gear, then wandered towards the open door where he found Hengest leaning against the post, gazing into the middle distance. Sigeferth was wresting the remains of a venison carcass from a serving lad, complaining that he hadn't finished with it. Frithuwulf was helping Eaha and some Jutes to bring in our weapons and line them along the wall. Some were still drinking, but most were aware of the tension that lingered from the evening. Many were weary, already settling for the night, wrapping themselves in their cloaks near the fire. After checking for my spear and shield I did the same, and found what pillow I could from amongst the furnishings. I, too, felt weary as I lay there and sleep gathered around me. The wind had died away and a clear night air gradually cleared the smoke and cooking smells from the hall. The quiet voices of Hnæf and Hengest murmuring to one another in the doorway just reached me where I lay. Hengest was speaking:

"I fear that I have entangled you in an ancient feud, my lord King. I had not wished to burden you with the troubles of my ancestors. Say the word, and I will take my men and go, and chance a passage overland."

"Nay, my friend. You gave me your allegiance, and that of your fellows, and I value it higher than you know. We face this as one."

Vaguely comforted by the young king's words, I drifted into sleep.

I awoke with a start, I know not how much later. The murmur of voices still drifted from the doorway, and I picked up Hengest's voice, suddenly more alert:

"Yonder light... I wonder what could it be? Too early for the dawn — cometh a dragon here? Do the gables burn?"

FRESWAEL

The Finnesburh fragment, part of a lay.

Hnæf spoke, warlike young king:
"Neither is this the eastern dawn,
Nor here dragon flyeth,
Nor here do this hall's gables burn;
But here forth bear mortal foes, men fully armed.
Birds cry, greyhame yowleth, spear clashes,
Shield answers shaft. Now shineth this moon,
Wandering under clouds. Now ariseth deeds of woe,
That this folk's enmity will bitterly end.
Awaken now, warriors mine!
Seize your mailcoats, think of valour,
Bear yourselves bravely, be resolute!"

Then arose many a gold-laden thegn, girding on his sword.
Then to the door went the noble warriors,
Sigeferth and Eaha, their swords drawing,
And at the other door, Ordlaf and Guthlaf,
And Hengest himself followed close behind.

Then to Garulf, Guthere spoke, exhorting him,
That in his armour he should not risk
So precious a life in the first attack on the hall door,
Now that a hardy warrior was ready to take it away.
But he cried over all the clamour, that valiant hero,
demanding to know who held the door.
"Sigeferth is my name," quoth he, "I am a prince of the Secgan,
wrecca widely known; many old woes and hard battles
have I passed through; and here is allotted

31

whatever fate you would seek from me."

Then in the hall was the sound of deadly conflict:
The hollow shield-board, the body's guard,
Burst apart in the hands of the brave;
The beams of the hall resounded,
Until in the fight lay Garulf, dead:
The first bound to earth, Guthulf's son,
And around him many good men,
The bodies of the brave.
Raven wandered, swart and seal-dark.
Sword gleams flickered,
As if all Finnesburh were aflame.

Never have I heard in any clash of foes,
Did sixty valiant warriors bear themselves so well,
Nor ever did a man's own companions
Make better payment for their white mead,
Than did his young warriors make to Hnæf.
For five days, so well they fought, that none of the retainers
fell;
Nay, they held the doors.

When a wounded champion turned away
Saying that his byrnie was broken,
His armour useless, and his helmet also pierced,
The folk's guardian[1] soon asked him,
How those other warriors their wounds endured,
Or which of those two young men...
....has from the fray turned...

---

1 Finn

The singer has taken licence, as singers will. We saw nothing of Finn during those days. His position was not to be envied. What he knew of the attack, or when he learned of it, I do not know. I cannot think that he would have consented to it beforehand. His own son was amongst our number, and we were in his own great hall, his invited guests. This attack trespassed on his royal *mund,* his right to enjoy peace in his own hall, and it certainly contravened any duty of hospitality. But we were privy to none of his counsel. We just had to fight for our king.

They kept coming to the doorway, reckless and raging, and there they fell. It soon became obvious that angry and determined as they were, these men had seen little enough of battle, had less idea of strategy, and had only their hatred and numbers to sustain their attack; unlike Hnæf and Hengest, who very quickly organized their battle, rotating the three or four men at the doorways regularly, taking full advantage of our defensive position in the hall. The attackers were unable to join shields, the front being too narrow. Those who attempted two at a time were met with a heavy axe — retrieved from the chest originally intended as Yuletide gifts for Finn — deprived of their shields and exposed, they too fell. And so it went on. Their plan was not working, and they seemed to lack the wit to change it: our plan was working, and we had no need to change it.

Within the hall, those of us not directly engaged in the battle made shift to provide what sustenance we could find. Hunger set in on the second day. The venison Sigeferth had rescued was soon gone, which left us searching for scraps of burnt meat from the fire and anything edible from around the benches. The fire was kept going with plenty of embers and unburned ends. Ordlaf had found some dry pease from the sea voyage in his scrip, and this, together with a broth we boiled from the bones and scraps in a shield boss, we made a kind of pottage, more or less disgusting to the senses, but it kept us going. A great earthenware water jar stood in one corner of the hall. When we were in the fight the mood of battle sustained us, but as we were relieved we could think of little but food. By the third day our strength was noticeably ebbing, and still they came. Gnawed at from within and assailed from without, we fought on, but this could not last.

My own turn at the doors had been grim. Shield and sword, one eye on the line of the threshold: never step over it yourself, but draw them over it if you can, feign to yield, sidestep and let the inner guards deal with them, then back to the threshold for the next. Use height, use the shield boss to thrust at their face, turn and upsweep with sword — knees, elbows, jaw, all became targets — turn and shield thrust again. The hatred that suffused their faces, the fury of their attacks betrayed them to their end. The yard before the doors was a scene of terrible carnage. They recovered their dead and wounded during the lulls between their attacks, and of course we did not hinder them.

It was turning colder. The wind off the sea had lessened, but swung east of north; a penetrating chill pervaded the hall. At dusk on the third day, the first flakes of snow had started to float through the eastern doorway. Hnæf and Hengest were sitting at one of the benches near the back of the hall, heads together. Hnæf was speaking:

"Finn must put an end to this — it doesn't make any sense."

Hengest considered.

"My lord, I think he will, but not before his Jutes have had their fill of vengeance, an account that grows by the hour as we cut them down. He has allowed them their head so far: they must have persuaded him of their case. And their case is against me, and our Jutes."

"What! You would still have me desert you? Or perhaps you would wish to leave me?"

"Nay lord, I am your sworn servant, to stay or go as you command. But I still think that Finn would allow you and the rest of your retinue to walk away from here, if he could then feed me and mine to his hounds yonder."

Hnæf raised his eyes to the doorway.

"As you say. But I will not be granting his wish. You and I are bound. Besides, it is late for such considerations, now that such a treachery has been committed. How can my sister bear this? The insult is to me and mine. He plays with fire."

Hengest idly dangled and swung between finger and thumb of his long hands the *francisca*, or Frankish throwing axe, that had come through a doorway the previous day, thankfully missing its target and embedding itself in one of the next row of wooden pillars — a weapon unknown to us, and one that he had taken a liking to, practicing at whiles by hurling it at the woodwork. Eventually he spoke:

"Our men are exhausted and starving, but they remain resolute, having come this far. And I have been counting. They have lost many, where we have not. The tally is now more even…"

Darkness was falling, the snow settling. The clamour and clash of weapons from the doorways had subsided, and an unfamiliar stillness descended on the hall. Men leaned against the wooden pillars, or on their weapons, or slumped down on

35

benches, their breath steaming in the chill air. Hnæf and Hengest arose and walked towards Eaha standing at one of the doorways.

"A respite. No tricks?" Hnæf asked.

"None that I can see, lord. Their sorties are fewer, the gaps between grow longer. Perhaps they tire — or perhaps they learn."

"Perhaps they learn. Turn the guard, get some rest. We will see what the dawn brings."

The dawn came after a quiet night with dark skies and the doorway ankle deep in snow. Men stirred, rising stiffly to their feet in the cold dawn. The fire had long since died, its fuel exhausted. I had been on watch since the small hours, and seen nothing. But now, across the courtyard before the eastern doors, there was movement. I called Hengest over, and we watched as, one by one, our enemies started to line up on the further side: tall and silent, each moved up to his place. Hengest had been right, their numbers were noticeably fewer, but this was still a formidable sight, and now amongst them we saw some of Finn's own Frisian warriors, men who, by their grizzled faces and scars, were no strangers to warfare. This was intended as a show of strength. In their silence they stared at us, still and forbidding. Hnæf joined us at the doorway. After a moment he broke the silence, his voice echoing around the courtyard.

"Where is the King, my sister's husband? For I would seek counsel with him!"

One of the Frisian warriors stepped forward. An older man, but massively framed and muscled, lengthy hair and long taches streaked with grey.

"I will convey your wish, when I am next at leisure. But first we have some vermin to dispose of. Yield up those men who once called themselves Jutes, and yonder captain, son of a king slayer, and the sooner you may speak with our king."

"You speak of my sworn companions. Until they unswear their allegiance, they remain mine, and I will yield none. Plague us with no further terms, for I will hear none, save from the lips of your king."

The big Frisian shrugged, turned and rejoined his fellows. The first onset was not long in coming. We bore it, but there was a renewed ferocity, and the presence of the Frisian warriors could be felt. We were beginning to receive more injuries as weariness took us. We were now mounting more men to each door, but the risk of getting in each other's way was increased. By the afternoon we were changing the watch far more frequently, and those not engaged were patching injured companions or snatching rest, slumped over the benches. The trampled snow in the doorways was a red slush, and the footing was treacherous. Darkness fell, and gradually the attacks abated. Exhausted men drank the last of the water, chewed on leather or dry bones, slumped to the ground rolled in their cloaks, save those on the watch. There was a sense that the morning would bring doom.

I awakened in the middle of the night. The moon was shining brightly through the doorway, revealing a fresh fall of snow. More snow was promised by the look of the great rolling clouds that threatened to engulf her. Stamping my feet and beating my sides to try to warm my blood, I wandered across to the doorway. Young Frithuwulf was on the watch with Sigeferth. Hnæf had been careful not to put him in exposed positions, whilst making sure that he took his part. He would always have an experienced mentor posted with him. Now he looked as though he was struggling to keep awake, but he seemed to appreciate an opportunity to take his mind off sleep.

"Is all well?" I ventured.

"All is quiet," he said, "although I would give much for a bite of bread and a warm cloak. Then would all be well!"

The moon disappeared behind the bank of cloud, bringing darkness and the first flakes of fresh snow. Something moved in the deeper darkness on the far side of the courtyard. Frithuwulf scraped at the snow beneath the great door with the butt of his spear.

"How will this end? My father must come. How can he just act as though none of this is happening?"

"I wish I could tell you. But I think the end will be soon, for good or ill… and then we will either look back at this time having defended our king, or joining our forefathers in the halls of the gods… Wait… something stirs… over there!"

"Be alert! Our enemies come! Brace yourselves!"

A clatter from the hall behind us as men groped for their weapons and shields. Our foes came across the courtyard in a column, spears raised, at a loping run, with a fierce growling roar, and crashed into the doorwards. Frithuwulf had been well drilled: a mirror to Sigeferth at the other doorpost, he absorbed most of the impact, shoulder braced to shield, then turned and sidestepped leaving the first rank of the attackers, still being carried forward by the momentum of their charge, to face Hnæf and Eaha as they entered the hall. Shield thrust at the man in the second rank, knocking him sideways, Frithuwulf pinned the tumbling man with a spear thrust, but his lunge had taken him over the threshold: the great javelin, wielded by one of the warriors they always sent around to flank the doorways, tore past the edge of his shield and took him beneath the shoulder-blade. The flanking warrior drew his heavy ash spear for a second thrust, but Hnæfs swinging sword took him under the arm, near severing arm and spear. Hnæf quickly stooped to haul Frithuwulf up, but he could not stand, and as he tried to drag the boy backwards, another spear took the young king in the gorget. King and nephew collapsed backwards over the threshold, and hands appeared to drag them from harm's way, but the attackers had not been slow to take advantage of the sudden gap. Surging past Sigeferth, their leaders were suddenly within the hall, and their followers were moving to secure the passage. In the near complete darkness inside the hall, the ensuing melee was hampered by the inability to distinguish friend from foe. A ring of shield-warriors surrounded the recumbent shapes of Hnæf and Frithuwulf in one dark corner, but the long frustration and vengeance of our adversaries was now upon us.

I managed to get hold of my gear and bash and hack my way back towards Sigeferth at the doorway: the sparks from the clash of weapons almost the only light to see by. Others sought the doors, and after a few minutes we had stemmed the breach, and heaving bodies and clutter aside, managed to get them shut and barred — we thought that there were now too few enemies without to break them down in a hurry - buying us precious time. By this time, someone had managed to kindle some rags as a torch, and we could gain some idea of the position in the hall. There were individual clashes everywhere: thirty or more of Finn's warriors had got in, and now stood between us and our stricken lord. The fighting swirled around the benches. The meagre light of the torch just marked the reflected bosses of the shield wall, and before it were clustered most of Finn's men.

Leaving as many as we could to defend the doors from those nearby, who were now realising that they were trapped, and attacked us with renewed fury, a few of us skirted the benches to relieve the shield wall. Driving in at the side of the attackers we managed to take the force from their assault on our comrades, and extend the line. But the fight was more open now that our advantage was gone, and both sides were losing men. Within the hall we now had the greater numbers, but just then a resounding *boom* resonated through the hall. A momentary silence fell, as men glanced over their shoulders to see whence this new threat came. A few moments later the thunderous noise sounded once more — something gigantic was hammering at the eastern doors. Thoughts of dragons again flitted across men's minds, by the sudden anxiety reflected in their faces. Again it thundered, and this time there was a tumultuous crash as the bars gave way and the doors fell in ruin. Backing away, the doorwards joined those on the west side to face whatever was coming in.

Picking their way through the wreckage, and around the tree trunk they had used as a ram, came Finn's closest retainers, bearing torches, fully armoured but with spears reversed, in sign of peace, and behind them the king himself.

"Enough of this!" he bellowed, and the lines drew back from one another.

"Where is my wife's brother? Where is king Hnæf?"

In the light of the torches, the full extent of the carnage was exposed. The floor of the hall was littered with the dead and dying. To one side lay the great wreck of the Frisian warrior who had spoken before the doors, a *francisca* buried

40

in his face. From the far end of the hall beyond the wall of shields, Hengest, mounting a bench so that he might be seen above the confusion, called with icy clarity down the hall:

"I see these men heed your commands, lord King; do they follow your bidding in all things? If it is our king you seek, Finn Folcwalding, you come late. My lord and King lies here lifeless, pierced by treacherous spears. He lost his life whilst aiding young Frithuwulf, who lies here stricken beside him, from the field."

As the colour drained from Finn's face, Hengest went on:

"Is this not the way it would always end? I know not whether you unleashed these hounds upon us, or just turned away while they broke from their bounds. One way or another, you did not call them off. And lately your own men can be counted within their pack. The peace of your court would be a jest if it were not such a matter of grief. What say you?"

Finn's gaze ranged over the shambles in the hall. He slowly turned to face Hengest.

"Your words are full of pain for me. As a father I have been to these men, as my father was before me. Their claim had substance, and I could not deny them. And now I have lost my son, and my wife's brother. But come, there has been enough killing. Shall we not speak together, you and I, as you seem now to speak for these warriors? They have fought valiantly, and now neither of us have enough strength to achieve an outcome. For my own, you are to withdraw — more than enough lives and time has been spent on your feud."

Amidst some muttering, the survivors of Finn's troop bore their dead and wounded from the hall. His personal retinue remained, whilst a table was set on the dais at the end of the hall, and Finn and Hengest sat down to parley.

FRESWÆL

From Beowulf

When the sudden peril came upon them,
The doughty Healfdene, Hnæf of the Scyldings,
In Freswæl his fall was fated.
Nor indeed had Hildeburh cause to praise
The Jutish loyalty. Without fault of hers she was
Bereft of of her loved ones at that shield play,
Child and brother. They fell by doom,
Wounded with spears; that was a sad lady.
Not without cause did Hoc's daughter
Her destined lot bemoan, when morning came,
When she beneath the light of heaven could see
The murderous evil among kinsfolk.
Where he aforetime had possessed the greatest
Of worldly bliss, there war swept away all
Finn's thegns, save few alone;
So that he in that meeting place could not
Fight out the battle with Hengest,
Nor wrest the survivors of the disaster from
The king's thegn. Nay, they offered him terms,
That he should provide another building entire,
Hall and high settle, that they half might have,
Sharing it with the sons of the Jutes;
And that at the giving of gifts, Folcwalding's son
Should every day honour the Danes,
And should gladden Hengest's troop even as greatly
With jewelled treasures and plated gold,

As he was wont to enhearten the Frisian race with
In the drinking hall.
Then they confirmed on two sides,
A fast pact of peace. Finn to Hengest,
Without cavil, with oaths declared
That he would honourably treat the remnant,
In accordance with his counsellors' wisdom,
That any man there neither by words nor deeds
Should break the pact, nor with malicious intrigue
Ever cast it up, even though they followed their ring-giver's
slayer,
Being princeless, since it had been thus forced on them.
If, however, any of the Frisians with daring remark
Should bring to mind the deadly feud,
Then the sword's edge should follow.

Pyre was made ready, and bright gold
Brought up from hoard. War-Scylding[2],
Best of warriors, was for the fire ready.
On that pyre was plainly seen
Bloodstained mailshirts, wild swine engelded,
Boar crest iron-hard, many noble lords
Maimed by spears. Some few had in that slaughter fallen!
Then Hildeburh at Hnæf's pyre,
Bade men commit her own son to the flame,
To burn him body and bone, and be given to the pyre
At his uncle's shoulder. The lady mourned,
Singing a sad lament. The warrior was mounted on the pyre.
Curling to the clouds, the greatest of slaughter-fires

---

2 A term for the Danes, in this case Hnæf.

Roared before the burial mound. Heads melted,
Wound-gates opened, then blood sprang out
at the cruel bite of flame. Fire consumed all,
greediest spirit, which there carried off those
of both folk. Their glory had departed!

The warriors went to visit the villages,
Bereft of friends, to look on Frisia,
Its homesteads and high citadel. Hengest still through that
Bloodstained winter abode with Finn
All unhappily; his own land he remembered,
Although he might not on the sea drive
His ring-prowed ship: the ocean with storm surged,
Striving with wind, winter waters belocked,
Icebound, until another year came to men's homes,
Even as they yet do, gloriously bright weathers that
Always observe their season. Then winter departed,
Fair was the lap of earth. The exile was eager to go,
Guest of the court. Yet he to vengeance
Rather thought, than to journey by sea —
Whether he a hostile encounter might bring about,
That he might in his heart remember the sons of the Jutes.
So he did not refuse the way of the world
When Hunlaf's son placed Hildeleoma³,
Best of swords, in his lap —
Whose edges were known among the Jutes;
So by the bold hearted, Finn was then assailed,
Cruel death by the sword, at his own home,
As soon as word of the deadly onslaught Guthlaf and Oslaf,

---

3 'Battlegleam'

After sea journey, had in their grief related,
Blaming him[4] for their share of sorrow: nor might the restless
heart[5]
Be restrained in the breast. Then was hall reddened
With lifeblood of enemies, so too was Finn slain,
King amid his troop, and the queen taken.
The Scylding warriors to their ships bore
All the riches of the king of the land,
Such as at Finn's home they might find
By way of figured jewels and cunning gems. They over sea-
lanes
the noble lady to Deneland bore away,
leading her back to her people.

---

4 Finn
5 i.e Hengest's

SÆLADE

Sea Journey

On a calm sea with a following wind, the rowing was easy. The constant pull in rhythm demanded little thought, leaving the mind to follow its own paths as we glided along within sight of the coast. We now had no pressure to keep up with the other ship, Guthlaf and Oslaf having parted company with us and the greater part of the spoils of Finnesburh, when they departed with Hildeburh for the north and Hoc's court. Hengest, now less certain of a welcome anywhere after his agreement with Finn, had chosen to seek another path. Our ships had been looked after, rather surprisingly, considering the want of hospitality shown to us in all else; the coastguard having perhaps reached his own view on the turn of events in Finnesburh.

Finn had furnished us with a lesser hall, but it was just as defensible, should the need have arisen, and as the snows had fallen and ice covered the ditches and meres, we eventually celebrated Yule in some kind of comfort, our new lord anxious to make amends for earlier shortcomings, and found time to salve our wounds and fill our bellies — and grieve for our lost. Memories of that fey and unsettled winter came and went as we rowed up the Frisian sea: the memory of Hengest, sitting alone on a washed-up driftwood log at the edge of the dunes, loose limbed, with head and shoulders stooped as his elbows rested on his knees. None dared approach him; save Guthlaf, walking out towards him, with Hnæf's sword Hildeleoma glinting in his hand. Hengest did not move as Guthlaf gently dropped the sword into his lap. But he tensed, as if a snake, not a sword, lay there. It might as well have been a serpent — a writhing link in the dread chain of vengeance. The inner turmoil was visible even from a distance, and for the first time I felt pity for him. Slowly his hand moved to its grip and he held it up, staring at the patterns of its forging, the runes chased on its bright blade, its edges gleaming in the low winter sun. For a while he was still, then the briefest of nods to Guthlaf, who withdrew. The die was cast. Only a pretext was lacking. In the end, fate dropped that into his lap too.

With the afternoon sun on our faces, we hauled between the islands and the coast. We saw a small fishing boat, whose men eyed us warily as we passed, knowing that we could easily overhaul them of we chose; but we had food enough. My thoughts drifted again: to Frisia. As time had passed, and the idea that we were now Finn's men filtered out, we were able to move around the burh with some freedom, and eventually to explore the hinterland. A party of us walked to the estuary where we had seen there were a number of boatyards. I watched as Hengest, normally a man of few words, overcame the shipwrights' natural taciturnity by showing a lively interest in their craft, eventually parting with each of them on cheerful terms. Walking inland, we crossed large fields of grain and pasture, and again Hengest persuaded a farmer to show him a great plough, hauled by eight oxen, and even got him to set it working, despite the season. We meandered back to Finnesburh past small hamlets, many of them on terps raised above the level of the marshes and coastal lands. A rich country, but here and there could be seen evidence that the sea was a constant threat; corners of creeks and ditches choked with driftwood from past storms, and the terps themselves, man-made islands trying to keep up with the rising of the sea, to keep a few inches above the next spring tide storm.

But as time had gone on, Guthlaf, Oslaf and the rest of the Danes had departed, and Hengest, Eaha, myself and the rest of our Jutes remained with Finn as the weather grew steadily warmer, and the fields and trees sprang into green life. But it was never an entirely comfortable arrangement; and the knowledge that a plot was afoot didn't make things easier for those who knew. One day, the storm broke. Finn had been at his judgement seat, hearing the petitions of his people, when one of the few Jutish survivors of the *Freswæl* stood and accused Hengest of a new crime, claiming that he had seen him frequenting Queen Hildeburh's quarters on several occasions. And having observed a visit once, he had gathered witnesses to subsequent sightings. Finn arose from his seat, looking as angry as I had seen him.

"Octa son of Whitgils, have you aught to say to this?"

After a moment's hesitation, Hengest replied:

"Naught, my lord."

"This is the last thing I had expected," declared Finn, cooling quickly.

"Guards! Send for my lady Hildeburh. Hengest, we had an agreement. How comes it that you should abuse the trust we pledged one to another?"

"I can say naught, my lord."

Hildeburh appeared between her escorts, graceful as ever, a slightly puzzled crease on her brow.

"Lady, this man stands accused of frequenting your chambers. What say you to this?"

Without hesitation, Hildeburh replied:

"That he speaks truly, my lord, but this is not as you imagine..."

"What! One of them will not deny his accuser and the other presumes that I use too much of my imagination when none is needful. Confine them both in fetters, somewhere out of my sight, while I consider their doom. This audience is ended."

As Hengest and Hildeburh were taken away, Hengest turned, and called:

"My lord King! Be not overlong in your consideration, as you were when we your guests were beset, lest your own doom overtake you!"

"Would you threaten me as well as injure me, boy?" Finn exploded, then, controlling himself, added:

"Hengest... you are valiant, but young. I may feel moved to overlook this abuse of my hospitality and spare your life, but kerb your tongue."

"Ha! Spare me your discourse on hospitality! We came here and found none. Kill me or spare me, I will dwell under your roof no longer."

"So be it. Take him away before I do something I might regret."

I, and several others started to move to prevent this, but Eaha signalled for us to remain still. As Finn left the hall, we looked at one another. Finn's own retainers were evidently wary too, as in ones and twos we dispersed. As we walked back to our hall, I fell into step with Eaha.

He spoke quietly, so none could overhear:

"The Danes are returned. Arm yourself. Find where Hengest and the lady are confined, and watch. No harm must come to them. The rest will move towards securing the gate. Do not delay!"

So I gathered my sword, concealed it under my breeches and made my way through the twilight, around the back of the great hall. Voices could be heard from a nearby building. Moving around the eaves I found a gap through which I could see. I saw Hengest, who was seated on a stool facing me, a foot fettered to a post; and, though I thought I had moved quietly, he was, disconcertingly, looking straight at me. He was speaking to a guard, who had his back towards me. The guard was mocking him.

"Hospitality to your liking now, my lord?"

"Bate me as you please, now. All will burn."

His eyes met mine again, and I understood. I crept away from my hiding place, gathered a pot of fat and oil from the door of the cookhouse and a flaming brand from a sconce, made my way to the darkest corner of the great hall, and cast the contents of the pot as high as I could up the slope of the dry shingles. I pulled a few handfuls of old thatch from the roof of a nearby building and laid them up the slope, then emptied the last dregs of fat on it before setting the brand to it. It caught quickly, and as I hurried back to the gaol building, I could see that the corner of Finn's great hall was well alight, with thick black smoke from the fat starting to drift and curl around the other buildings in the slight breeze off the sea.

I waited a while to make sure the fire had taken properly, then taking a deep breath, I yelled:

"Fire! The King's hall is afire! Quickly, someone, fetch water. Fire!"

Returning to my spyhole, I saw Hengest's guard go to the doorway, curse, and run from the place. I ran round and through the door.

"Have you a blade?" he asked.

"My sword."

"That post — as quickly as you may."

"If I had thought I'd have brought that bloody great axe," I said, as I started on the upright, avoiding the metal of the ring bolt. Down stroke, down, upstroke, up, down, down. The sound of more running feet could be heard outside — people running past towards the fire, but all that was to be seen by anyone glancing in was Hengest sitting on his stool. At last the notch grew to a great bite from the wood exposing the metal within, which could be prised out and he was free. Stuffing the chain up his breech leg and winding it round his belt while I checked the way was clear, we were both up and out of the building.

"Come, we need to find the lady Hildeburh. I think they may have taken her back to her own rooms. Where are the rest?"

"Gone to the gate. Eaha sent me."

"Have you another weapon?"

"No... but take my sword. Shall I fetch that axe?"

"Yes, do, and a shield and my helm and... my sword might be of use. I will meet you at or in the lady's rooms."

I ran back to our deserted hall around the backs of the lowhouses, hastily wrapped what was needful in a tunic, and

51

bolted back the way I had come, round the last corner and straight into the arms of one of the King's household warriors.

"Ho! Steady there," he said. "What errand takes you with such haste?"

"The fire! I have brought axe, tools to save the hall!"

The orange glow now silhouetted every building. And from the direction of the hall, there now came other sounds, the clash of weapons and cries.

"Come, bring that axe, something is afoot. The hall will have to burn."

We both took off towards the sounds, but I fell behind and dodged into an alleyway, then switched back towards the queen's chambers. The guard had abandoned his ward to attend the alarms, just as Hengest's had, and there I found him, in earnest conversation with the queen. Her serving woman, who I recognised from that first fateful night in Finn's hall, had been allowed to attend her.

"But what is happening?" she cried, "and why did you not tell the king of your reason?"

"Your people are here," he replied, "they come to avenge many wrongs."

"My lord the King? No! It cannot be! You made a peace. Is it not enough that my brother and my son have been taken, that you will take my husband too? Tell me this is not to happen, please… it must not… You… you have brought this doom. Why did you ever come here?" she sobbed

"I would not have chosen this ending, lady," he said, "if I had not had to watch the death by treachery of so many valiant men. Your husband did nothing… nothing to prevent it. And now he will pay… and so will others."

He signalled me forward, and I took the axe from its wrappings, and set the helm, shield and the sword that I had found amongst his gear on a table. Hildeburh had been bound in the same way as Hengest, and I reached for her chain. The smith had left his hammer and a cold chisel by the door, to collect later, so I gave the axe a mighty swing and lodged it deep in the top of a bench. The lady started when I did this, and again when I reached for her wrist.

"What are you doing?" she cried.

"No harm, my lady. I intend to cut your chains. The fire will reach here before long, and it were well you were not here."

I set to work on the shackle, using the axe head as an anvil, while Hengest was conversing with the maidservant.

"Gerutha, come with me," I heard him whisper. "They will love you not, when they discover the truth."

"What? And go a-roving with you, Hengest?' she replied. "No! I will not leave my people, whatever they may say of me. Go, and good fortune be with you, and maybe it will one day bring us together once more?"

"Such would be my wish," he replied, and they kissed. Then he went to the table, girt on his sword, helm and shield.

"Take them to a safe place, Æschere, our hall might be best, and stay with them until this is finished. I will see you there. Now go!"

I loosened the axe and we went, staying in the shadows of the eaves, winding our way from building to building. The folk were out, all running towards the fire, intent on the alarm, and few marked us. When we reached the hall, we found two of my people there finding fresh arms. They said that the gate had been taken, and the Danes had streamed in; all Finn's men, both Frisians and Jutes, had withdrawn up the hill to defend the king. I grabbed what I could for myself, a shield and a spear, and persuaded them to guard the women for Hengest, then returned the way I had come. Moving between the cookhouse and a store house, I found Hengest.

*

I mused as the motion of the ship, gliding across a glassy still sea, in the warm glow of a setting sun, with the occasional murmur of voices was a balm seldom felt. The tensions of the times I relate were gradually ebbing, and the relaxation of the steady pull on the oars created a contentment I recognised would not last for long. But it is good to think, and recollect what has happened, and order the mind. Glancing over my shoulder, the coiled rings of the serpentine figurehead led us on through the smooth sea, towards a fate of which we knew little as yet. But having handled what we had, we felt that we could manage almost anything.

I returned to my recollections of *Finnesburh*, for I had not finished the retelling of them through my mind. I remembered finding Hengest with his back to me, silhouetted against the distant glow of the flames. Facing him was Guthere, the old spear warrior I remembered from Finn's hall, and three other Jutish warriors who had survived the *Freswael*.

"So, Angle, you shed your chains just in time to meet us. I thought that this truce could not last. Even now our king will brush off this treachery as one would brush off a gadfly."

"Our king, Guthere? I'm sure it has been very convenient to shelter under Finn's wing up until now, but things have changed. You speak of treachery, but I know who it was who

54

stirred up young Garulf to lead the attack on us — the same who, realizing he'd overplayed his hand, tried to stop the young fool from throwing his life away. How long had you been poisoning his mind with tales of grandeur? Have you at times ever stopped to think of the cost of your words and actions? No, I think not. Well, think now, for payment for your treachery is required of you: payment in full."

"As ever the Angles are stuffed with words before they fight, when they seem so quiet the rest of the time. But come, the odds are in my favour, this is hardly fair — but... Oh, yes, I was forgetting... you folk prefer it that way; so let us get on."

With that he bore down on Hengest with his shield before sidestepping and aiming a murderous thrust at his side, which Hengest only avoided by rotating his body forward. I could not watch, so I grasped the great axe, stepped out from the shadow of the eaves, and brought it crashing down on Guthere's shield, cleaving it to the boss, where it lodged, and I wrenched it away from his grasp.

"Stand away!" Hengest hissed at me as he cast away his own shield. Both of them being shieldless, there followed a lightning-fast exchange of blows and parries, but Hildeleoma found its mark, and Guthere crashed in a heap against the wall of the alleyway, choking in his own gore, and rattled his last breath. As the next pair came on, I took up position beside Hengest as he recovered his shield, and we ran up the alley to meet them. Shields crashed together, but our weight was evenly matched. I managed to take two rapid steps backward and swing my axe up left-handed in a diagonal stroke before he could recover his balance. It shattered his shield and the elbow beneath, and he screamed as his good arm swung at me with his sword. I parried it with my shield and smashed it into his face and he went down to his knees. I hit his head sideways with the flat of the axe and he stopped trying to get up. Hengest had dispatched his man, and then we heard Finn's familiar great voice calling to rally his men, and the remaining Jute turned and ran to join his king.

For the rest, it was as the scop related: Hildeburh had managed to elude her wards, and my last memory was of her running to her dying husband amid the bodies of his retinue, and cradling his head in her lap as the life left him, and her despairing cry. They put his body on a byre and walked him, at Hengest's insistance, with some honour into his burning hall, before raiding his treasury and the final dash to the coast.

*

The wind began to freshen from the sea, and the rising swell demanded more of our concentration as we pulled for Fifeldor. As we crested a ridge, the lookout spotted another craft pulling in our direction.

"Another keel, pulling hard… a war band, Saxon, I think, out of the Elbe river. They will be up with us before the mid-day."

"All hands to the oars, then, that we might have more time to gauge their strength!" Hengest cried.

As the morning wore on, the wind and waves subsided a little, and our pursuers had gained considerably, and were now in plain view. Our losses in that final attack on Finn's hall now told against us — we were not a full crew, and could now only man two and twenty oars out of the twenty-eight positions. And what was worse, the lookout called that another ship had he sighted, pulling towards our path to cut us off.

"They know what we carry, Hengest," shouted Eaha the steersman.

"Aye, news travels fast over land. Pull hard, my warriors."

Our share of Finn's hoard was contained in two long cases stowed beneath the rowing benches, resting on the ribs in the middle of the ship. More weight to slow us down. Hengest shipped his oar and called for me to do the same, our positions being opposite. Between us we opened the cases. Many gemstones there were, and marvellous accoutrements. Hengest picked out the finest from both cases and wrapped them in a large piece of cloth, tying it to a length of rope before concealing it beneath a bench. Of what remained, he cast a half over the side, making sure that the Saxon warriors could have seen, but without being too obvious. The remaining half we spread evenly between the cases and returned to our oars.

"Eaha, steer us a straight course for freedom. When that keel ahead blocks our way, make to veer away, then turn to ram them. Now, let us put on all that we have, pull... pull... pull!"

As the other ship swung in front of us, warriors poised in her bow ready to board, Eaha made his feint, appearing to swing away into a parallel course, but almost immediately steering back into the other keel, assisted by the port-side oars. We still carried some speed from our final pull, and there was a tremendous crash and splintering of oars and timber as our bow ploughed into the other ship, throwing the Saxon boarders off balance, two of them into the sea, others falling back into their vessel. Grappling irons snaked over toward our gunwales but the one that did strike near the bow was quickly cut with a sword.

"Pole away, and pull for the open water!" yelled Hengest, "Eaha, that island yonder to the north. Pull!" and we did. There was some confusion on the Saxon boat, for they did not immediately respond, and when their sweeps eventually struck a rhythm to follow us, there were fewer of them. I think they were occupied with pulling their fellows from the water, but judging by the activity near their bow, our attack may have holed them. Unfortunately it seemed that it had also damaged us, as our feet were now being cooled by a body of water swirling back and forth with each stroke of our oars. We had sprung a plank in the bow, and the sea was rushing in as the front oarsmen rushed to block the hole with whatever rags and clothes they could lay hands on. Even so, we had put a good distance between us and our enemy before they managed to sort out their pursuit, and even then they gained little in the next hour.

We continued our course towards the distant low island, but by this time the first of our pursuers had overtaken their fellows in the wounded vessel. Still they gained on us, and before long they were within arrow-shot. Hengest ordered the first of the cases to be slung overboard. It just about managed to float, and we poled it out as far from our wake as we could. It made us a little lighter, but it engaged our enemies wonderfully as they tried to lay hold of it before it could sink, and gained us a little time. Ever Hengest encouraged us:

"Pull, men, pull, and maybe the gods will grant us some dry land to fight on!"

Before long, the Saxon keel was gaining on us once more, but now we could see the distant shore getting closer as we glanced over our shoulders. We could see that the tide was near the full; but at this rate they would catch us before we could drive our stricken ship on the sand. The water was now halfway up our shins and the ship began to wallow noticeably. We poled out the remaining case but it didn't make much difference to our way. Again our enemies paused while they fished for it, but from the groans of disappointment they must have lost it to the deep, whilst we gained precious yards. A furlong from the shore, Hengest slipped our bundle of remaining treasure over the side unnoticed, before resuming his oar and shouting:

"Now! Pull for your lives!"

A few more yards and we felt a slight heave as the ship touched the sand, followed by the grind and shudder as she settled, twenty yards from the shore. We grabbed our weapons and shields and vaulted over the side as the Saxon keel shot past us, landing further up the surf, not being so low in the water.

It was a different kind of battle, up to our knees in the surf, an individual melee, as warriors faced one another in a dozen desperate struggles near the water's edge. They outnumbered us, but not overwhelmingly so; though that would change when their second ship managed to gain the shore. Hengest fought with restrained ferocity, two dead or wounded Saxon warriors lay already before him. As I engaged my opponent, I noticed from the corner of my eye that the second Saxon ship was no closer, in fact they were trying to hail their comrades on the shore, pointing and gesticulating to the north. I saw my opponent glance over my shoulder, and disengage, backing away behind his shield, and suddenly they were running for their ship. I looked behind me and there, having just emerged from behind a dune headland, there was a ship, under a sail, lined with shields. The Saxon warriors heaved their ship off the sand and leaped aboard, grabbing their oars. They had their case of treasure, and had seen from our wallowing wreck that there was no more to be had, and the prospect of gaining a few slaves to go with it suddenly lost its appeal, so they pulled for the sea before the newcomer could come up. We watched as they took their fellows in tow and swept for their home shores. Some of us pulled the wounded from the water, and we made our way up the surf to the strand and subsided with exhaustion. One of the Saxon warriors who had been left for dead still breathed, and we squeezed the remaining water from his lungs, dressed his wounds and bound him. If he recovered, he could man an oar as well as another, and we had lost one of our own in the fight.

The ship lowered its yard and the great sail collapsed to the deck to be bound up by the crew. Sweeps were run out, and the vessel edged towards the shore. Two men leaped down from her into waist-deep water, and waded through the surf to the strand. The taller of them strode up to Hengest where he sat on a tump of short turf in the sand at the edge of the dune.

"Well, what a day of wonders!" he exclaimed, "a knackered ship watched over by a knackered stallion!"

A slow smile spread over Hengest's features, the first I had seen for many a day.

"How now, brother... and well met!" he said as he stood to embrace the man who was by no means his twin, but seemed more and more like him the more one saw them together.

"My brother, Ebissa..." Hengest introduced us.

"What! All Jutes?" declared Ebissa, "I'll get a crick in my neck looking up at you lot all day. Ah well. Ah... Eaha! Someone I can talk to on the level. You look well, if slightly bloody."

"All the better for seeing you, lord," Eaha replied, "your arrival was well timed."

"Hmm. Yonder sea-wolves have been lurking about these waters for a couple of days, now. Mayhap they were waiting for something. I thought it might be interesting to find out what — or who; and what do I find? What have you been up to, brother?"

"We carried treasure from the sack of Finnesburh. They must have heard of it — I hadn't thought that word would travel with such speed. We used some of it to delay their advance. Some was lost, some they recovered; and some we may regain, with patience."

"So," exclaimed Ebissa, "we have some waiting to do. Tell me, for I have heard of a famous defence of a Frisian hall by a young Danish king and his retinue, particularly of the part played by a certain Hengest, and how they came to terms with their host. But how comes it that I find you as fugitives on this island strand?"

"A long story, brother, but first let us deal with the dead. Have you any swimming fish amongst your crew?"

"One or two."

"Mayhap you might take your noble craft beyond the surf, about half a mile out, along this line..."

He drew a straight line in the sand to indicate the direction,

"...and find, if you can, a wooden case, which our pursuers failed to collect."

The tide was now turning at the full, and as Ebissa returned to his ship, Hengest bade us find driftwood enough to build a great fire. As the afternoon wore on, the tide receded and a vast expanse of sand was revealed. A joyful cheer from

Ebissa's ship spoke of a successful dive, and from a great distance we could just make out the shape of the second wooden case being hauled up the side on ropes. When we had finished building the pyre the sun emerged from a bank of cloud and we walked down to look at our poor ship, now aground and leaking a steady stream of water back onto the sand. Ebissa had returned with many of his troop, and he eyed the beached vessel.

"We could probably repair it enough to get it home to our yard, the winds being kind," he mused. "I'll send for some tools and my boat swain; and something to eat. You must be hungry."

A few of us stayed to finish bailing out the ship and help with the repairs. We gave our fallen comrade to the fire as evening came on, together with our dead enemies. At a separate fire we cooked the salted pig that Ebissa had brought from his ship, now a distant shape beyond the expanse of sand, and feasted as darkness fell. Hengest had wandered down the sand to collect his bundle of Finn's treasure, now almost buried, rinsed it in a pool and brought it back to our encampment. After a song and setting the watch, the rest of us rolled up in our cloaks and slept where we were, for we were bone weary from that final dash for the shore and the ensuing fight, but heartily relieved that help had come unlooked for.

We awoke to a glorious sunrise. As the tide made its way back in again our ship floated again, now with its sprung plank levered back in and only slightly cracked, bandaged and caulked, and we rowed gently clear of the surf, and set off after Ebissa's craft with its glorious sail. By evening we were waiting for the tide to gain enough to carry us past the renowned Fifeldor and up the Eider river, then upriver to moor by a jetty on the northern bank. There was a yard, and another new keel a-building under an open-sided shed. The old shipwright had come out to watch as we moored. He sniffed, then spat, and sniffed again.

"As if I haven't got enough troubles already' he muttered.

From WIDSITH

...Witta weold Swæfum...
...Offa weold Ongle...
...merce gemærde wið Myrgingum
bi Fifeldore: heoldon forð siþþan
Engle ond Swæfe, swa hit Offa geslog.

Witta ruled Swæfe... Offa ruled Angeln.
He drew the boundary with the Myrgings
by Fifeldor: Angles and Swæfe held it after,
as Offa struck it out...

King Wihtgils' court was settled at a modest hall not far from the coast. The king came out to meet us, embraced his son, and, ignoring formalities, beckoned us all inside. Calling for food to be prepared, and ale to be brought forth, he settled us all on the benches. His lady came forward with the cup to the king, then honouring Hengest and moving on to each of us. I have seldom felt so truly welcomed, and later, when Hengest, Ebissa and the king were close in conversation together, the men around the benches were relaxed and laughing, it occurred to me how little of this side of life we had enjoyed for so many moons. I should have known it would not last. We slept in comfort that night, but after we had risen on a breezy morning, two horsemen approached the vill. One of them dismounted, calling for audience with the king, leaving his mount with his companion. As he strode towards the hall Ebissa addressed him:

"Ho! Cousin! What's the rush? Look who is here!"

The newcomer stopped as he lay eyes on Hengest. Ebissa pressed on:

"Well, isn't this fun! Three horsies together! A stallion, a Famous Horse[6] and a humble one. Shall we ride together?"

"Idiot! Where is your king? I must speak with him."

"Ah. That's the trouble with kings, never around when you need them. Truth to tell, we had a bit of a late night, and he might still be abed."

"Oh, send him in!" boomed the king's voice from within.

We could hear a little from outside. There wasn't much to hear.

"Well, lord Eomær, what brings you here so early? We have been celebrating my son's return."

"Lord King, I bring a message from my father. He demands to see Octa, your son, at the earliest opportunity."

"Come now, he has just returned from strenuous ventures. I am sure he will come to pay his respects before long."

"My father commands that he return with me immediately, Lord."

"What? So soon? You would deprive me of my son so soon? I have seen so little of him... very well. Hengest! Come to your father... Your cousin here demands that you go with him to see the king of the Angles. You had better do so. But

---

6 Eomær = 'famous horse'

see that you return quickly! I had forgotten my pleasure at your company. Fare well and speed back to us."

"I will, Father, but first I would bestow these gifts," and he fetched the bundle of remnants from Finn's treasure house. The king's eyes widened at the gleaming gold and jewels that spilled from the old garment.

"You are a good and dutiful son. But should these not be taken to our overlord?"

"I think the high king will not be disappointed by what I set before him. Farewell, Father."

As he emerged from the hall, Hengest sent for another horse. They found one, more of a pony, and he bade me strap the treasure case to it. Then he mounted the horse left by the other rider, who was to remain at Wihtgils' hall until Hengest returned before reclaiming his mount — a reassuring sign. He turned to Eomær:

"I would bring my trusted retainer, to guard this treasure."

"As you will," Eomær replied, and Hengest nodded to me to mount the poor pony, which I just about managed with one leg draped over the treasure case. And so we trotted off across the fields and heathlands. We kept up a brisk pace and there wasn't much converse between the two cousins. I had the sense that there was a tension between them. Eomær seemed constrained by some knowledge that he would not disclose, and Hengest kept his own counsel, as usual.

In the middle of the afternoon we rode down from a low ridge covered in birch trees towards the royal seat of the Anglekin, where King Angeltheow son of Offa held sway. The enclosure was very much larger than Wihtgils' modest hall, with practice grounds, stables, a smithy and smelting yard, and farm buildings without, where all manner of beasts could be seen, heard or smelt. Despite the summer sun, the day was quite cool, and the smoke of several fires arose from the hall, the cookhouse and the smithy.

I tied up my pony to a tree and detached the straps of the treasure case from her back whilst Hengest and Eomær dismounted and handed their reins to stable boys. Hengest bade me follow them with the case, but only bring it forth when called for, and we made our way up the low steps to the royal hall. As we entered the gloom from the bright sunlight without it took a while to make out any of the features within. The long hearth lay before us as was usual, and we turned to the right to be confronted by several figures whose countenance we could only just make out in the dim firelight. The figure seated in their midst spoke:

"Ah, Octa. You have come. Thank you, Eomær, we will speak together later."

"My lord King," said Hengest, bowing, "I have wandered far since last I beheld your royal splendour. I now bring you gifts as a token of my esteem."

He signalled me forward and I lay the case of treasure at the feet of the King. King Angeltheow, son of the renowned King Offa, greying hair in plaits framing his lean and slightly haggard face, glanced at the precious gems, the arm rings and brooches, without moving.

"I am glad, young man, that you have not abandoned all sense of duty. Yet I hear of a story from the land of the Frisians that fills me with great concern as to the honour of my house, and therefore yours also. This is why I required your presence here. Now tell me how came the mighty King of the Frisians to be laid low?"

Whilst Hengest related our tale without adornment, I watched the old king through the layers of woodsmoke that drifted and swirled through the dim shadows of his hall, lord of a mighty people, and was filled with foreboding. He had not brought Hengest here to commend him on his bravery and wisdom — so much was evident from his face, with its tightly drawn lines, grizzled taches and grimly taut mouth. When Hengest had finished, King Angeltheow spoke:

"An interesting tale, and yet I find that it prompts a number of questions in my mind. Tell me, what does honour demand of a thegn, in war?"

"That he fight to defend his lord... and, cometh that time, to die with him."

"And yet here you stand before me, still quick, your Lord Hnæf having been killed."

"I had yet to avenge my Lord Hnæf," Hengest replied, "and the ability of either side to continue the fight was in the balance. To spare further bloodshed, I consented to terms."

"This was not, then, to save your own skin? For that is the feeling I have. Now having come to terms with the murderers of your lord, you lived at peace with them for many months, and dutifully served your new master, you say, and enjoyed his hall and mead, meat and gifts and all the other benefits thereof. Yet suddenly you betray the trust and the truce, and treacherously conspire in his undoing and death, breaking that pact of peace. Tell me, sir... Does this sound honourable to you? Is this seemly conduct for a prince of the Swæfe?"

Hengest was quiet, but I could sense the tension building within.

"Your silence does you no credit. Speak out!"

"Very well, lord King, I will speak. Much did I listen and much did I learn in Frisia. I will speak of a time, many years ago, when a proud people sought to govern themselves, and what is more there emerged from their noble ranks a man of such bravery and craft and wisdom that the people, by public acclaim, elected him as their king. The ruler of a powerful neighbouring kingdom, however, claimed that this people, of whom my retainer here is one, had no right to proclaim a king, and he found excuse to invade their country and murder their king, subjecting his people thenceforth to foreign rule. What I learned, to my cost, in the land of the Frisians, was the extent of the resentment caused by those events, and the hatred borne us by those of them who could not bear to live under such tyranny. Your father, my lord, King Offa of great renown, was so sensitive to a wrong committed in his people's name, that he remained silent and unspeaking until an opportunity came whereby he could cancel out that wrong, and restore the honour of his people. I have to ask, since you raise the subject of honour, whether or not the Jutish people are not also the victims of an ancient wrong at the hands of our forefathers? For myself, I defended my lord and took vengeance on those whom I knew to be the cause of his death."

During this speech, King Angeltheow's face seemed to grow ever darker and more tightly drawn. At times he would signal for one or other of the figures who stood around him, members of his *witan,* his ruler's council, to whisper to his ear their advices. When Hengest had finished, a tense silence fell in the hall. Then the King spoke:

"Octa son of Wihtgils, I think I have now heard enough. You seem to hold a strange sympathy for those who have attacked and killed your lord, and you have presumed to

68

compare your motives with those of my father, King Offa, to whom you bear, as yet, little comparison. You have also suggested that our people are guilty of tyranny, when in fact the Jutes have always been our peaceable subjects and allies. Amleth's uprising was little but a brief aspiration to greater things. One day you may learn of the burdens and expediences of rule. But you will not learn it here, nor in any of the lands where we hold sway. A man who makes a fast pact of peace one day and betrays it another is not a man who we could trust in our counsels. I therefore declare you, Octa son of Wihtgils as *nothing*, and you have a sevennight to leave these lands. Thereafter any man who finds you may slay you out of hand without *wergeld* and without reprisal. Now be gone from our presence."

Hengest turned after the briefest of bows and strode from the hall. As we left the doors, the stern glances of the groups of fighting men followed us back to our mounts, yet there was no abuse, no jeering, and I felt no particular animosity from them. Hengest was, after all, one of their own. I cast a leg over my pony, aware that my feet hardly cleared the ground and we rode away. It must have been a comical sight, yet no mocking laughter followed us as we rode back up the heath. And as the evening sun set behind the low horizon, we returned to the hall of King Wihtgils.

WRECLĀST

Path of Exile

The pale owl quartered the fen as King Wihtgils' entourage threaded its way along the narrow path through tumps of sedge and coarse grasses, and the last light of day brought us within sight of the king's northernmost hall. As the sedge gave way to shorter, sheep-bitten turf, we emerged from the fen and dismounted to lead our horses into the enclosure, where some lads were waiting to take them off to the stables. I had been found a mount that matched my size a little better than my last pony, but I was unused to riding for a whole day and felt stiff and aching, and even envied the others of our troop who had elected to walk, and were still trailing over the fen behind us.

The hall was a welcome sight. The king's stewards had lit a fire and set some food in preparation, and ale was brought in from an undercroft, and we settled in for the evening. But we were not a happy band. On the second day since our return from King Angeltheow's hall, the uncertainty about our future affected everyone: we were still within the lands held in sway by the mighty king of the Angles, and Hengest's days of grace were ebbing away. Eventually the ale began to improve our mood. Whatever happened, some kind of action would ensue. We were therefore a little surprised by what came next.

The king eventually stirred from deep thought.

"My son, I do not pretend to understand the mind of my cousin King Angeltheow; I strongly feel that some of his witan are craven old fools who spend most of their time recalling an age of romance and grandeur that never actually happened, whilst forgetting that some of the family's deeds have been far from heroic. But however I might disagree with him, I must abide by his judgement. We have not the might to challenge him here. My people enjoy a peace that is precious enough in these days. So I have to ask you, what do you intend?"

"My lord King," Hengest replied, "the king of the Angles' judgement is applied to myself, and none other. My men have served me well and honourably, and I intend to send them to their homes in the North." At this there was a deep rumble in the hall, such as one might hear from the throat of a hound sensing a threat.

"For myself, I will be *wrecca,* and pursue my fortune on further shores. By your leave, my father King, in three days' time, I will return to Fifeldor and my ship, with any who wish to follow me."

"But where will you go?"

"I… do not know," Hengest replied, "but I have yet three days to ponder upon it."

We crossed into the land of the Jutes the following morning. Those who lived further north were lent horses. My home was only half a day's march from the boundary, and I was still suffering from the previous day's ride, so I declined the offer. My father's farmstead, clothed in its verdant midsummer richness, brought back many memories of my childhood, and there was my mother, feeding the hens, looking little changed from the time when I had left her to seek my fortune with a prince of the Angles, in the great Danish court of the Hocings four winters past.

She was surprised and pleased to see me, and her eyes lit when I showed her the jewelled pendant I had brought her from the treasure of the King of the Frisians. My father was more concerned as to whether I was staying until the harvest, for an extra pair of strong arms would have been very welcome, he said; and he was only slightly mollified by the gift of a dagger and golden sheath bejewelled with deep red stones when I said that I could not stay, for my lord had further need of me; for the more I thought, the less I could see myself following a farmer's way, and I had been drawn into another life entirely.

And so, on the third day, I bade my parents farewell, and walked back through the wetlands to King Wihtgils' northern hall. As I entered the doors, there seemed to be many more men at the mead benches than had departed three days before. Nearly all our original band were there; and there were some youths of both Swæfe and Jutes who no doubt had heard of Hengest's exploits, and seen an opportunity to join the following of such a renowned warrior; and there was a handful of more experienced men, who were prepared to take the known risk of joining a following led by an exiled man. The problem was that there were more men than could possibly fit on Hengest's ship. Mead and ale were flowing freely, and there was a hum of excitement in the hall. Hengest was deep in converse with his father, who looked gravely concerned. Looking around the hall I had an opportunity to size up some of the hopeful young men who would have joined us. Some seemed very young, though tall of stature. Some were full of words, others more circumspect. From time to time, Hengest would signal for the serving men and maids to circulate with more drink. I felt a surfeit already, so I made my way out into the cool evening air. The last light was disappearing in the western sky, and the sky was clear and full of stars. Across the fen the ghostly shape of the pale owl, gliding, hovering and diving, was accompanied by the unearthly screech of tawny owls from further away on the fen's fringe. They have a kingdom, I thought, and rule the night. And now we have none. I was about to turn and make my way back to the hall when something moved on the low horizon, a shadow in motion. A rider, moving at as brisk a trot as the ground would allow, making for the hall. I turned and ran back to the hall as the horseman rode up and dismounted, taking the horse's bridle as he thanked me and walked briskly into the hall. Moments later he emerged, speaking with Hengest.

"I come from my lord Ebissa," he was saying. "He bids me tell you that two men have arrived by Fifeldor, inquiring after the warrior known as Hengest.'

"What manner of men?" Hengest replied.

"One tall, seemingly a Jute; the other a weasel. They arrived on a trader, and claim to come from the land of the Britons. Ebissa bids you to come, to discover their business, which they say they will disclose only to you."

"I thank you for your message. Now come and join us, you must need refreshment. In the morning I would have you bear a reply to my brother, but rest for now in my father's hall. But wait… know you aught of my ship? Is it yet repaired?"

"I spoke to the shipwright yestereve. He said that it was badly wrenched, and that it was more like to fly than swim. But you know what he's like. He's been working on it."

"Please to inform that old goat when you return that Hengest will have need of it in two days, and if it is not ready by then, he will be the one doing the flying."

The messenger smiled.

"Aye, my lord. It will be my pleasure."

I went to find a boy to stable the messenger's horse, then wandered back to the hall. The king had heard enough of all the rowdy noise and retired, a signal for an end to the merriment, and men were wrapping themselves in their cloaks and finding what space they could on the hall floor. I picked my way over their recumbent bodies to find my own space, and fell asleep soon after laying down, despite the noise still coming from the most drunken of the revellers.

We were awoken by a tremendous din, the clamour of pots and shields being beaten, and loud voices demanding that everyone muster at the practice ground, an area of level horse-bitten turf beyond the buildings of the royal vill. Ebissa's messenger rode off into the fens. It was still dark, with a faint radiance beginning to suffuse the eastern sky. Some were still too drunk to walk, and were left where they groaned or slept. Of those who made it to the ground, bleary eyed and full of sleep, Hengest's veterans were bidden to defend a post with a horsetail pennant in the centre of the field. All were armed with staves and shields. The warriors who aspired to join us were commanded to attack and capture the pennant.

Despite the missing stragglers, the odds were still over two to one, but the first attack was pitiable; men who moved gingerly, with too much care for their aching heads, and making no inroads into the ring of shields. Hengest watched from a slightly elevated tump by the stockade, whetting his sword the while. The second sortie was little better than the first, and the attackers were being awakened with smart blows from the defenders' staves. This seemed to do the trick, as the more nimble-minded of them started to consult and form a strategy. Choosing a point on the circle, they charged it with a shield-tipped wedge, and ignoring the blows, forced their way forward and started to roll us apart. Another party flanked around the circle, preventing us from reinforcing the front. We consolidated as best we could, but before long they reached the post and bore off their prize to Hengest on his hill.

Hengest had seen what he wanted to see. He selected the men he wanted, sent the rest home along with the drunks in the hall, and told us that we were leaving in an hour. In his hall, while we bundled up our gear, he spoke to his father the king:

"My lord, I am determined to voyage south and west; I will return to the land of the Frisians."

"But why? You will hardly be welcomed there, of all places."

"Where then will I be welcome, Father?"

The king sighed, and his head dropped.

"So be it. May the goddess show you her favour, and protect you from misfortune… and may I live to see you again, my son. Fare you well."

They embraced, and Hengest walked from the hall to mount his horse. As the sun rose, we trudged back through the fens.

Later that day, we emerged from trees to see the king's southern hall bathed in early evening sun.

"Brother! I see you have been hunting for men!" declared Ebissa as we gathered by the hall and saw to the horses. "Come, I am afire to learn what these visitors are about, but they are tighter than clams."

"All in good time, Horsa," Hengest replied. "First, I would know the state of my ship."

"Well, the shipwright has been strangely busy since your message arrived at midday, but he had not been idle before that. Another day should see it floating like a duck on Eider.'

"Another day is all I have."

"Calm yourself brother. I've seen no sign of Anglian assassins since you've been away. Come! Let us go and pretend we are kings, for the benefit of these guests from afar. You, lad!" he called to a youth, "Bring us a table and some mead, and then go and call the men of the Britons."

I was among half a dozen of the better equipped of Hengest's men to serve as a guard of honour, and we took up positions at intervals down either side of the hall holding ashen spears. Before long, two men were escorted into the hall. The first was plainly of Jutish origin, tall, high cheekbones and a broad brow. The other only came up to the first's shoulder, a narrow man with a narrow face, a wispy half beard, and small yet busy eyes. They bowed as they arrived at the table.

"Welcome, sirs," said Ebissa, "I make known to you my brother prince of the Swæfe, Octa son of Wihtgils, son of Witta, son of Wehta, son of Wihtlæg, son of Woden."

The skinny man replied, in a language that seemed harsh and gutteral, yet not without music. The taller man spoke in our own tongue, but with a slightly strange accent:

"My master names himself Guuin. I, Ecgberht, speak for him."

76

Mead was poured. The skinny man, Guuin, spoke again, and Ecgberht translated:

"My master says that our lord, King Vortigern of Britain, has bidden him seek a warrior who walks by the name of Hengest. King Vortigern has heard remarkable reports of this man, and wishes to make a proposal to him which will be to his benefit."

After a short pause, Hengest said:

"I am he. Say on."

There was another exchange between the two men, then Ecgberht spoke:

"In former years there has developed a custom for the men of these lands to find proud service in the ranks of the armies of the Romans who have fought in Britain. Indeed, such men have earned great renown in such service, and been highly valued by their new masters, earning rich reward. My king now has need of such men as never before, to fight the enemies of his people, who harass his shores with attacks of growing boldness and savagery from the land of the Picts... amongst others."

Hengest regarded them steadily, but said nothing. More words flowed between the visitors.

"Our King's especial need is in the provision of ships and men who are adept at warfare by sea, and may oppose and chase down these raiders. My master bids me offer you high status in the employ of his king, Vortigern: yourself and up to a hundred fighting men, and the ships to carry them. For this he will pay in gold and provisions for your men."

Another silence, then Ecgberht added:

"This is the offer of the King of the Britons."

"You speak of enemies other than the Pictish people," said Hengest, breaking the silence. "What others?"

The Briton spoke to Ecgberht, with a slight hesitation.

"Some Saxon raiders... pirates and the like..."

Hengest frowned.

"And...?"

"There is... another ruler, in the south of Britain, who contests King Vortigern' supremacy, but he is of little account. King Vortigern controls the major part, except for the mountainous areas of the north, whence come the Pictish people."

"So you would require me to fight upon two fronts, north and south?" Hengest replied. "No, I think you have wasted your journey, sirs. If I need gold and provisions, why should I bow to serve an unknown lord? Why not join the Pictish men, and the Saxon pirates, and help myself by plundering your coasts?"

There was a hurried, heated discussion between the two men. Then Ecgberht spoke:

"My master says that he has heard tell that you might yourself find difficulty in finding a base for such activity, as, and please forgive our temerity, your fame has not left everyone with a favourable impression. Are we not correct in thinking you an exile in your own land?"

Ebissa glanced at Hengest, but he seemed slightly amused by this ploy.

"Sirs, it is true that I am an exile, and few would welcome my presence. But before I give you my final answer, let me speak alone with Ecgberht, for I know his people and would know a thing before I decide."

Ecgberht translated this, but his fellow refused to agree to it, gesturing angrily.

Hengest just shrugged:

"Then my answer must be no."

So Guuin unhappily agreed, and Hengest and Ecgberht went outside together. Luckily my position by the door allowed me to just overhear their conversation.

"This king, Vortigern," said Hengest. "Does his name have a meaning, in the tongue of the Britons?"

"I should not say, lord."

"Why not? This negotiation depends upon it. Come, speak."

"In the tongue of the Britons, it means 'proud tyrant', lord."

"Thank you. Let us return."

Guuin was deeply suspicious of his colleague when they arrived back at the table, and there was a hissing exchange between the two men.

Hengest considered for a few moments, then spoke:

"Sirs, I have considered your offer. You lay claim to the heritage of the Romans, but I fear that they have long since abandoned you, as is well known. I know little of your king or your country, and from what I have learned, I would be committing myself and my men to joining a sinking ship, which I will not do. I regret that your journey has been wasted, but I cannot accept your invitation. I wish you a safe journey to your home."

I watched as the colour drained from the Briton's face. Hengest had risen from the table, nodded to the men, and was walking towards the doors. Guuin hissed a torrent of words at his companion

"Wait!" cried Ecgberht, "there is land..."

Hengest paused.

"What land?"

"We... neglected to mention... our master has empowered us to offer you land, a considerable island, by the coast, as a base for your military activities."

"The name of this island?"

"In the British tongue, Ruaim; some know it as Tanatos."

Hengest resumed his walk towards the doors, calling, "Please to wait for my return!"

He went out into the forecourt, and called as many to him as were in the vicinity of the hall.

"Do any of you know aught of Britain, and of an island called Tanatos?"

"Aye, lord. I have been there."

It was our Saxon who spoke. Having recovered from his wound, he had been released from his chains, showing no inclination to run, and had become a part of our troop, although he had yet to be trusted to bear weapons.

"We went on a raid there once. It lies in the mouth of the Stur river, and has marshes on that side, cliffs and shingle and sand beaches on the other. Some woods, some fields, some sheep pasture on low hill. A man might walk from one end to the other and back in a morning: its breadth in half that time. It is faced by two of the Roman shore forts, at either end of the channel that parts it from the main. Many ships may lie sheltered in that channel.'

"The Stur river, where does it lead?"

"To the stoneburh the men of Rome called Durovernum of the Cantii, lord."

"I thank you, Ulf," said Hengest, and returned to the table in the hall. He sat down.

"Please to tell your king that I will come. But I will need time to prepare. He should expect me before winter closes the sea lanes."

After the agreement had been sealed with mead and Guuin and Ecgberht had departed, Hengest and Ebissa remained for a while.

"Hard bargaining, brother! I do believe you wrung them dry."

"The Briton was crafty. I wonder if his master is of the same mould."

"No doubt you will find out soon enough. But why the delay?"

Hengest swirled the last of his mead in the cup.

"There is something I need to do first. I return to the land of the Frisians."

"You are, of course, a madman."

Ebissa stood up with such force that the chair clattered to the floor behind him, and he started pacing up and down.

"If it's men you need, just say so. I will join you, yes, and my ship, and my men. We could make up a small army just like that. Why go to Frisia, where they will string you up as soon as look at you?"

Hengest sighed.

"My brother! Of course you can come: but not yet. Father needs you here. I will send before I need you, but you must trust me in this. Now I must get provision for my ship. May I draw from your stores?"

Ebissa pouted.

"Suppose so."

Again we drove our ship down between the coast and the islands. We made good time, and encountered no enemy. One day as we were pulling across an undulating sea, I was sharing a bench with Eaha, and as we rowed I told him of Hengest's journey to the court of King Angeltheow, and what had happened there. Eaha, an Angle himself, listened attentively while I told the story. When I had finished, I expressed my puzzlement at the reasons the King could have for losing Hengest, and all his abilities. Eaha thought for a few strokes of the sweeps before answering:

"You have met Eomær, the king's son, have you not?"

"Yes, I have."

"How would you appraise him?"

"Proud, inclining to arrogant."

"Ha! Just so. They are a proud line of a proud people. So, when such a king perceives that a warrior of a junior branch of the family has performed a deed of great renown, a deed greater than any of his own or his son's, he may grow envious. He might also worry that such a man might present a threat, if allowed to linger too close to home, especially if, as you say, Hengest has suggested that there is some unredressed misdeed of his ancestors that he intends to dig up. But there is something more. My lord Angeltheow is no fool. He sees something in Hengest that is more than fighting quality, more than bravery, more than the ability to make men follow him. He sees in Hengest *destiny*, and has enough fatherly love for him to push him towards that destiny. So be not too quick to judge him harshly, for he is a wise and far sighted man, for all his pride."

"As are you, I deem."

We now had some forty men, enough to have relief watches again. Of Hengest's surviving troop, all had returned, and Eaha and the other Angles of our troop had stayed by Fifeldor since we first arrived there. To this score of men were added those who had been recruited from the Jutes, a handful of Swæfe, and the Saxon, Ulf. We continued to make good speed, but there were signs that the weather would not last. The horizon was a mass of majestic clouds underlined by darkness.

"Ulf!" called Eaha. "Tell us more of Britain."

"I was on a raid," declared Ulf, "not a sightseeing trip."

"I crave your pardon! Tell us anyway."

Ulf grinned and continued:

"We rowed up along the coast going westward. We passed the island Tanatos, then a boat shot out from the river there beneath a stone fort, and chased us, but we lost them in fog. When the fog cleared, we found ourselves in what must have been the mouth of a great river, for we could see islands and land on either side. We turned south for the land, where we found a fleet, a creek that ran some way inland. When we could float no more, we hid our boat in reeds, and walked through the marshes until we came to houses, many of them, some of stone. Furnaces and kilns were there, belching smoke and fumes, and the sound of smiths at work. We raided one of the stone houses near the edge of the village, and found much of value, but the alarm spread quickly, and armed men surprised us. We ran for our ship, but lost three of our men, ridden down by warriors on horses. Six of us made it back and we got our ship away, but they pursued us down the creek, and we lost another man to arrows. Luckily for us the fog came back down and hid us, and we escaped. But with only five oarsmen, we had the hardest pull for home of my life."

"These horse warriors — did they dismount to fight and draw bow?" asked his neighbour.

"Nay, not for a moment. I think they were guiding their horses with their legs, and had a strange saddle, leaving their arms free to ply their weapons. We were fortunate that the last dash to our ship was over wet reed swamp, where the horses might not venture, else none of us would have lived to tell the tale."

"A useful tale it was; my thanks, Ulf," said Eaha.

We rowed on in thought. The bank of cloud in the west loomed larger, obscuring the sinking sun, and we felt the wind freshening, and the swell rising. Some of the weather-wise were muttering amongst themselves, and Hengest changed our course for the line of islands to our north.

The first squall nearly stopped us, and brought with it a shower of stinging rain as the sea rose and the waves became more threatening under the darkening sky, running us up to their churning summits then down into the next valley. We had to fight to keep the ship facing into them as we crabbed towards the nearest island. At intervals one of the breakers would hit us diagonally, spilling water into the waist of our ship, and the relief watch were kept busy bailing it out again. The current seemed to grow ever stronger, until we were fighting to make any headway at all. At last we ran through a maelstrom of conflicting seas that threatened to swamp us, and into slightly calmer water as we rounded the tip of the island. We rowed until we found the best shelter we could, behind some dunes, before running our ship up the sandy strand. The tide seemed to be at the full, but we secured her with long lines

— just as well, because some hour later she was afloat again, as the spring tide grew higher and we had to haul her clear of the crashing waves, up to the very edge of the dunes. Now the rain really started in earnest, and we huddled down in our cloaks amid the dunes, finding what shelter we could in the dark, but there seemed to be no escape from the deluge.

When morning came, the worst of the weather had rolled inland, although the sky threatened more to come. The rain had stopped, and our ship was high and dry under the dunes, but seemed to have suffered no harm. We broke fast with some dry cheese as our clothing dried in the wind. While we were waiting for the tide, Hengest stood before us and spoke of the invitation of the Britons, and the necessity to recruit more men.

"I hope to find such men in the Frisian lands. This may not be easy, for obvious reasons. I could be recognised as the betrayer of their king, Finn Folcwalding, and many of you likewise. So our approach needs to be careful. Guard your names, or use other names, but name me not if you value your skins. We will land in small parties, as migrants from Jutland. I may disappear from sight for a while, and the better known of you also. We will venture inland, but you all need to make yourselves useful, if not invaluable, to the people there, before we embark for the land of the Britons as the leaves fall.

"I know why you joined me: as a leader in war, and to war I will ultimately lead you. But first I need your patience and your good judgement, in order to win the means to perform our enterprise. Are you willing to follow me in this?"

And to a man, we answered:

"Yes!"

Then someone started incanting

"Hengest... Hengest... Hengest..." and it spread to a deafening roar. Hengest raised his arm for silence, and the chant abated.

"First we need to win a peace."

As the next tide, even higher than the last, edged up to the dunes we heaved our ship into the surf, and resumed our course for the mainland. Around the middle day the sky darkened again and the rain started to fall in blinding torrents. The wind was less savage than on the previous day, but a rough sea made rowing hard work. As evening approached, we drew closer to the coast, passing the headland that we recognised from our previous landing, and continued along for some distance before edging in to put the first party of half a dozen men under Eaha down. Using what knowledge of the lie of the land we had gained earlier in the year, we had arranged meeting times and places at various intervals over the coming months, but there was an air of anxiety about this whole affair, for few of us could anticipate with any confidence how things would go.

We put out again and moved westward along past another headland, then a range of dunes and a bar before turning south to the mouth of the estuary we had seen from Finnesburh. Through the sheets of rain and the gloom it looked very different. There were trees, the occasional roofs of buildings, and now and again the remains of a village emerged from what was left of the *terp* on which it was built. But these emerged from a vast mere, its waters almost as disturbed as the sea itself. We could just about make out the line of the banks of the estuary, but we kept well out in the middle of the river. As we rowed up the fleet, the banks grew slightly closer, and we passed more terp settlements, all seemingly abandoned, except the one that wasn't. Rainwater and tide were meeting to cause a flood that must have been exceptional even for these flat lands, for the force of the currents was undermining and eating away the edges of the mound, and the tide was still making. A great tree trunk had stoven in the bow of a small boat at the edge of the mound, and amidst the ruin of the buildings, something moved. In the failing light it as hard to make out, until its head turned to look at us and gave a mournful bellow. The cow looked resigned to its fate, but Hengest changed our course to take a closer look. A child's figure stood to see what the cow was about, and, seeing us, called for his father. Hengest handed the steering oar to the nearest oarsman, bidding him gradually put us in close to the bank, and called for a man in the bow to gauge the depth with the notched spear shaft. We edged in towards the bank, here bereft of vegetation and all but invisible below the surface, but could go no further. The man hailed us, saying that there was a short causeway between the bank and the terp. Our oarsmen struggled to hold our station, whilst Hengest and I tied a line about us and gingerly lowered ourselves over the bow into the water. When it had reached our waists, I found the top of the bank with my foot amidst the swirling current, and was just about able to stand. Gradually we felt our way along the few yards of bank to the causeway, although the current was constantly threatening to dislodge us and pitch us into deep water. As we reached the terp, two more children and their mother had emerged from the ruins. They were soaked and bedraggled, looking anxious and uncertain, but as we clambered up onto what was left of dry ground, the eldest, about seven winters old by the look of him, took a step towards Hengest.

"Sir, please can you save our cow?"

Hengest looked at him.

"Maybe — if she can swim!"

He turned to the father.

"We need to leave now. This tide has a while yet to run, and it has been raining upstream for a good while. As they meet, your terp is like to disappear."

The man nodded reluctantly. Hengest picked up the younger children, one on each arm, and started back towards the ship, while I took the older on my shoulders. I tied the last two yards of the line to the man's waist, and he carried his wife in similar fashion, and we edged after Hengest along the hidden path. The water had risen noticably, and the ship was in danger of riding up onto the invisible bank. As we reached her there was a bigger gap than we remembered, and we teetered on the edge before the ship came forward, and strong arms reached down and hauled the children and their mother and father up the side and into the bow.

Hengest glanced my way, as if to ask 'are you willing to do this again?' I nodded, and we picked our way back towards the drowning terp. Now the current pulled more strongly than before, but now we knew where the route lay, we could tread it with more confidence. We reached the terp and I went to untie the cow, and lead it to the water's edge, whilst Hengest disappeared into the outbuildings. After much squealing and squawking, he emerged with his tunic tied as a sack over his shoulder. A pink snout poked out of an armhole. Tied with a leather thong by their feet round his neck three hens flapped and complained. In his arms was a smallish soaking-wet hound with long legs. I had started trying to get the cow to move into the water, but it was understandably reluctant to face the swirling currents. Hengest followed behind, slapping its rump to drive it forward. Eventually it fitfully started and stopped, and then allowed me to lead it when it found solid ground beneath the water. We got as far as the river bank when it stopped and refused to move any further, so I untied my line from my waist and fastened it to the cow's halter, before wading the last few yards to the ship and climbing aboard. But Hengest was now stuck behind the cow. Eventually we had to use the ship to pluck it from its perch into the stream, where it found its swimming legs, then edge backwards and inwards to pull Hengest from the bank. The farmer and his family, cold and wet but full of thanks, sat together in the well of the ship. The children's faces lit up when Hengest set down his burdens in their midst. He left the young pig and the chickens in their bindings, the hound with the eldest boy, and resumed a seat at the oars, stripped to the waist with his rank black locks sticking to his shoulders. The tide was still running up river, but with less force now, and we heaved at our oars to make as much headway as we could before darkness closed in, while the cow swam in our wake on the end of its rope.

After a while, at the height of the tide, the current abated, and we came to a broad bend in the river, and recognised on the north bank the shipyard we had visited in the spring. Here the bank was elevated to some height, and the open-sided sheds still emerged from the flood, and behind it the cluster of buildings where dwelt the shipwright and such men as served him, the whole village now an island. We touched the hythe to put Hengest ashore, and watched as he made his way, unarmed, up the bank to the low houses, while we tried to pull and pole the exhausted cow around until it had found a footing and staggered onto the shore. After a few moments, Hengest returned, and beckoned us in to the bank. We gratefully ran the boat up alongside the building and moored it.

Following Hengest's example, we left most of our arms in the ship, whilst we got the farmer and his family bestowed in an outbuilding, and our men in another. The shipwright was a hospitable man, and lit a fire beneath a thatched awning in his yard, firewood being in good supply to one of his trade. We brought some of our remaining supplies from the ship, and set about drying ourselves and our belongings, and preparing some supper. Hengest called me over and we went in to the house of the shipwright, where we were seated by the hearth while his wife found some extra bowls for the remnant of a stew they had eaten of earlier.

"So! Hengest…" declared the shipwright, "I had not thought to see you again so soon. Tell me, what fell need drives you back to our beleaguered land? I would guess that you know that your welcome here may be a mixed one."

"Yes… I know it," he replied, "and I come at great risk, I know, to myself and my men, but I am the more grateful for your hospitality because of that, for I also put you at risk for sheltering us, Swithræd."

The shipwright waved this aside. Hengest continued:

"So, depending upon your discretion, I will disclose my plans. We are a war band, but we mean the men of Frisia no harm. We will divide into small groups, and disperse. We come as migrants, to work for bed and board, as many have come from the land of the Jutes already. I am outcast from my native land, and can no more return there than I can find a welcome here. I do, however, have a purpose in hand, for which I will need more men. I have been invited to the land of the Britons, to fight for their king, one Vortigern. In return I have been promised land — the island called Tanatos.

"It would seem to me that a blood debt is owed to your people for the slaying of their king, whatever else may have come to pass before or after."

The fire danced shadows on the walls of the house behind them as the older man regarded Hengest intently over his beard. Hengest met his eyes.

"That debt," he said, "I would repay."

FOLCESWYRD

People's Destiny

"My thanks, friend Hengest," said Swithræd the shipwright, "for your honesty. Now tell me how you think I can be of help. I am but a humble shipwright."

"I had hoped that you might tell me of how things stand in Frisia, since I… departed."

The older man considered for a while before he spoke:

"First I must say that I don't get to hear of every whisper that passes around the countryside, but I do have some sources. I speak to folk who I meet in the course of supplying my timber, some farmers, and the seafaring traders who I meet by the nature of my profession.

"The sack of Finnesburh and the death of the King was noised far and wide within days. There were few enough of the King's retinue left after the *Freswæl*, but those who survived withdrew to a hall further inland where they endeavoured to secure the succession before any other pretenders appeared. Frealaf, the King's second son, had been away at a Frankish court beyond Rhine river since he was six years old, and even now has only seen thirteen winters, but was recalled and now sits on his father's throne. He is wise for his years, and is assembling a growing *witan* about him. He will need that support in the coming months.

"From what I can glean, there are mixed thoughts amongst the folk about the events in Finnesburh. Some resent the loss of their king and his son deeply, and blame their loss solely on you and your friends. Others say that the king brought disaster on himself by allowing his Jutes free rein. Yet others see treachery on both sides, and shrug it off as the outworking of many feuds. Whatever is thought, I would say that you would be well advised to lie low until you can gauge the situation with more certainty.

"As for our land, it is in trouble. There is little enough of it here to go around. Your band of 'migrants' here may be seen as yet another burden on our ground, to add to the constant flow of people from the Jutes' land and most of the other lands in between. The Franks press in on us from beyond the Rhine river, and the Saxons from the east. And now we have this deluge from the sky. People say that we have lost the favour of the gods. We are accustomed to floods, and have learned to work around them, but we have seldom seen aught like this, and never so early in the season. Much of our land is in the grip of the sea, and our crops are beaten down or washed away. There will be a thin harvest and, I dare say, disease will follow soon after the waters abate. This will be a hard winter.

"And yet we can still trade. Our ships may still ply the seas for profit from goods, even though few of those goods will come from here. Mayhap we will recover before long. We are a resilient people, and the land is fertile when not under sea. Such is the extent of my rede."

Hengest finished his stew and set down the bowl.

"For which I thank you, friend Swithræd. I have three and thirty men. We need to reach the nearest dry land before we eat you out of house and home. Have you a small boat?"

"Aye, there's a light skiff that will take a dozen men at a pinch, and some punts with shallow draft. But I could use some extra hands here, if you can spare them."

"Yes — of course, thank you; and my thanks to you and your lady wife for your hospitality. We must speak again in the morning, before we leave. Good night!"

We made our way out into the darkness and the incessant rain. Under the awning the firelight was reflected in the faces of the few of the men who remained into the night, murmuring amongst themselves, while most had retired to the outbuilding to sleep. Cloaks and other garments hung from the beams and eaves, steaming in the warmth of the fire. I went straight to our den and found a space in the straw. I fell asleep as soon as my head touched the ground.

The morning sun arose through gaps in the clouds, and everywhere the sound of water dripping from the eaves was the only sound to be heard. The tide was slightly lower than the last but we were no less isolated. I was to stay at the shipyard with a handful of the others; a dozen men would take the skiff back to the sea and south to the next river estuary. Hengest would take some men eastward in a punt, and the remaining men would cross the river to the nearest dry land, wherever that turned out to be. When they had all departed we set about securing Hengest's ship while the tide was still high. We watched as it receded over the course of the morning, revealing a landscape of mud, with uprooted trees and shrubs festooned with grass and reeds, and eventually the river banks and other features started to emerge. As the waters abated a little more with each tide, we spent some days helping to repair some of the damage to the stricken countryside. Eventually the ground was dry enough for the farmer and his family, and such of his beasts that remained, to make their way north across the soggy ground towards their own *hām*, where their relatives would be anxiously awaiting news of them. We looked across the flats to where their terp had been, but could make out no trace or remains of it.

Over the weeks, when we were not working away, we fell into the routine of the working day at the yard. We had few skills in working wood, but knew our way round a ship, and our time at the oars meant that every one of us was fit and strong. One day Swithræd was showing me the new keel he had in hand under an awning at the top of the bank. As he explained the various parts and processes, I commented on the difference in shape.

"Just so," he said. "Your ship is good for rowing through calm waters. It is long and narrow, like a knife edge, and cuts through the waves, giving little resistance, which aids the oarsmen. But what happens when you face the greater waves?"

I thought for a moment.

"The waves start to break over the side, much so in the middle ship."

"They do indeed. But our ships spend much time in the open sea, where there are no islands to scurry off to when a storm threatens, so we build them with more rounded bottoms, more like a milkmaid's hams, yes? This makes the ship ride on the waves rather than through them, so we have to do less bailing. This one may mount a sail, so we have made the keel heavier, to help hold the mast and sail upright."

"You trust Hengest?" I ventured, seeking some reassurance that this man, whose people we had assailed, would not betray us.

"Aye, I do, and have done since we first met. I still know little of his secret thought, as, I dare say, does any man. Yet I believe him when he declares his purposes. I know not the nature of the agreement he had with our king, but knowing Finn as I did, I would guess that he took some things for granted that perhaps he shouldn't have done. And paid the price. Hengest is a doughty warrior and leader of men. As a leader of men, he can foresee what they will do next, and foretell events."

"Can you foretell events?" I said.

"Me? No! Why should I need to? The ways of kings and thegns are little of my concern. I foresee that the floods will go, and maybe come again, the sun will go down and rise again, and I will wake up tomorrow and there will be more than enough work to do. Speaking of which, I have a task for you. A shipyard needs timber. Two of my men go up river tomorrow with a boat to fetch oak from the den. They will need two more hands to help, so take one of your men. I will need the rest here."

I woke up to the cockerel's call and the first light of a fine morning, broke fast on some of the delicious bread the shipwright's wife had just baked, and begged her for some provisions for the journey. I found Heathuweald, a strong young Jute from the new recruits, and went in search of the shipwright's men. Our boat was small, having four oars, and we were soon pulling up river with the tide, with the rising sun at our backs and a light mist swirling tendrils of white in the light airs over the flats before us. Before long our progress slowed as we reached the limits of the tidal flow, and we had to start rowing against the sluggish movement of the river. A heron fished in the shallows, and many geese gleaned amongst the detritus of the river banks. Ralf, one of the shipwright's men, started a rowing song in a low and rhythmic voice, that seemed to merge into the deep tranquility of the scene. Rowing through this strange land, with its huge skies and great expanses of mere, put me on mind of the benefits of peace, and of occupations other than fighting; how would it feel to be a fisherman, or a shipwright, a woodsman or even a swineherd? As I thought, we started to pass through stands of trees that eventually merged into a dense wood on the northern bank. After a short while we came on a short timber quay jutting out into the water, and we moored our boat to it, unloaded some gear and ropes, and made our way up the bank. Odda, the other shipwright's man, set off walking upstream, while the rest of us shouldered the gear and set off along a narrow ride into the woodland.

The path wandered much. Now and then we passed alongside areas of coppice, where banks and fences of hazel and ash had been thrown up against the deer who loved the young stems. Eventually the path reached the edge of a clearing of recently felled timber. There were stacks of faggots bound with bramble stems and poles of oak and ash of about twenty years, and lying on bearers, two straight oak standards a yard wide at their butt. Ralf showed us how to set about riving the oaks apart using wedges driven into the rays at the ends of the log with the back end of an axe, and opening the split further with a froe. Before we had gone far, Odda arrived with a pair of stocky ponies, harnessed for hauling, and set about hitching the first load of oak poles to them. He beckoned me over to give him a hand. These trees were less than a foot wide, and we loaded two at a time. We set off back down the ride towards the river, Odda leading the ponies who carried the front ends of the logs whilst I guided the skidding back end of the loads around the tighter corners with a rope tied to their ends. As the sun rose to midday, we emerged from the wood and unhitched the logs by the riverbank before setting off back for the next load. When we got back to the clearing, Heathuweald and Ralf had riven the first great log, and were now occupied with splitting the two halves in twain again. We stopped for some bread and cheese washed down with some ale, then returned to our task for the rest of the afternoon.

As the sun started to go down, it became noticeably cooler. We had shifted four more loads, as much as we could for the day, and Ralf made a fire while the ponies were unharnessed, fed and settled. I went off to gather more firewood, not unhappy to explore beyond the clearing. I ended up walking quite a way, gathering hazelnuts and berries as well as some longish boughs of deadwood. The sounds of evening surrounded me: a chorus of blackbirds settling to roost, some jays scolding one another. And another sound: singing, a woman's voice, pure and clear. I crept carefully toward the sound through the boughs and brambles, and then I saw her. Tall, fair, lovely, her hair braided in a silken rope down her long, straight back; and, very noticeably, with child. In a slight hollow in the wood, a great oak had blown over in some gale long past, and now leant slantwise on bent and shattered elbows; its vast root-plate formed the roof of a meagre wooden hall, which had been embellished by some human hand with sticks and a thatch of sedges to form a weatherproof shelter.

The whole place had the air of a sacred grove. I crept closer,
to hear better her lament:

I this tale tell of my sadness,
my own lot. I who may say
what troubles I endured since I grew up
new or old, never more than now
ever the torment I suffer of my exile's paths.

First my lord went hence from his people
over the rolling waves; I was anxious before dawn
over where my people-leader in the lands might be.
Then I set out, sought to follow,
friendless exile, because of my woeful need.

It befell that a man's kinsmen plotted
through secret thought that they might separate us
that we two be most widely sundered in the world
to live most wretchedly, and I pined.

My lord king commanded that I be brought here.
I have few friends in this place,
loyal friends — and so is my mind sad
that a man I thought most suited was found ill-fortuned, sad
spirited,
whose heart concealed scheming and murder.

With blithe countenance full oft we two vowed
that naught would part us save death alone.
Now is that unwoven, is now as if it never were,
our friendship. Now shall I far and near
my dear one's feud endure.

They bade me dwell in this wooded grove
under the oak tree in this earth cave.
Old is this earth hall; I am all longing.

Dim are the dens, higher the downs,
old forts, where biting briers thrive,
joyless dwellings. Full oft am I cruelly assailed
by the absence of my friend. There are friends on earth,
loving and living, they have their beds
while I at dawn walk alone
under the oak tree, around this earth cave
where I must sit the summer-long day.

Here I may weep, for the ways of exile are mine,
many hardships. Therefore I may never
from heartbreak find rest
from all this longing that in me this life begets.

It may be that my young man be sad of mood,
painful his heart's thought. Likewise also,
with blithe face he may, within his breast,
be of constant sorrows a host. Whether on himself alone
depend his earthly joys, or whether he is outlawed
in a far country; that my friend sits
under a stony slope, rime encrusted by the storm;
my friend, sad-spirited, surrounded by water,
in sad abode. This friend of mine may endure
an aching heart — it may be that he
remembers too often the joys of life and home.

Woe is to the one who must wait
for love to come from longing.'

As the song ended on a long, low note, I stirred, and stepped forward into the clearing.

"You are not without loyal friends, lady, even here."

She turned toward me, her face surprised and confused, and then ran up and threw her arms about me.

"Æschere! It is so good to see your face! But how come you here?"

"I came with Hengest to Friesland, with his followers. We are come in peace as travellers in search of an honest living. But our true purpose is to gather men. Hengest intends to cross the sea, to fight for the king of the Britons."

"But this is madness!' she declared. "Why here, of all places?"

"I am still not sure," I said, "but I believe… I believe he seeks redemption for past wrongs, and I think he seeks for you. How comes it that you are not with your people — are you really here alone?"

Gerutha looked down.

"He spoke truly… when they noticed that I was with child, they questioned me… I had to tell them. Now they think that Hengest consorted with me and the queen, though I told them it was not so. I was brought before our new king, and there was one amongst them who had survived Finn Folcwalding, his lord. He persuaded the young king that I should be banished to this place, so here am I. Æschere, why did I not go with him when he asked?" she said, through tears. "Why was I so foolish? I thought I would be in his way, entangling him."

"But how can you live here? You have nothing…"

"I manage. The woodsman who keeps the horses brings me food. I find nuts and berries, and water."

"This is no way to live, and you with child. You must come back with us."

"But they will find me!"

"We are staying at Swithræd the shipwright's yard down river, and will return there tomorrow with timber. The master knows our purpose, and has helped us. You will be safe, I will ensure it."

She returned to her hut, found a few precious things and a woollen shawl, which she wrapped around herself, and we made our way back through the wood as the darkness fell, and tawny owls screeched. A mist was rising, and to one side we heard a grunt and the cracking of branches as a boar rooted in the gloom. At last we saw the glow of a fire, and walked the last few yards to find a pot of hot stew boiling above it, and Ralf, Odda and Heathuweald telling one another stories. They broke off and looked up as we stepped into the firelight.

"Æsc!" said Ralf, "we were wondering whether to come searching — but I see we need not have troubled. Do you have women hidden anywhere else?"

I ignored the jibe.

"This is Gerutha, Hengest's friend. I found her in a wood hall up yonder. She must return with us for her safety, if that seems good to you."

There were nods of assent:

"Our pleasure, lady," said Ralf.

"I hope I may not be a hindrance to you, sirs."

"We are but simple men with rough manners, lady, but I hope that we will not offend. You are welcome here."

They sat her on the log near the fire, where she sat in silent thought whilst we busied ourselves serving the stew. Odda offered her a bowl and she ate hungrily. After a while she set down her bowl, thanking Odda.

"I thank you, sirs, for your hospitality, and I wish that you may not regret it. I am an exile in my own land, and I beg that you will tell none of my whereabouts."

"None will discover it from our lips," they reassured her, and she bade them a good night, wrapped herself in her shawl and found what space she could beside the log to lay down. Weary after our day's work, the rest of them did the same. I had the first watch, so I found a stump to sit on, and settled myself to think. As I stared into the darkness, at the far edge of the clearing a lean, dark shadow paused to sniff the air. I recalled the old saying:

For the grey one there has to be dread...nor indeed will it weep for the death and destruction of men, but will always wish for more[7].

For an instant a pair of yellow eyes were reflected in the firelight; then the creature caught the scent of men and loped away into the wood. How had Gerutha survived in such a lonely place? Was it a sacred grove? Did they worship Nerthus here? She was evidently resilient. And what had she said about the man who had persuaded the king to condemn her... a survivor of the *Freswæl*, evidently, though King Finn's retainers we had thought to be all slain with him. The chain of vengeance was not ended, then, and for us, the hatred of men was more to be dreaded than the beast I had seen slipping away into the trees a few moments ago.

The moon emerged from clouds, now well past the full, and illuminated one side of the clearing, an intricate pattern of

---

7 Maxims 1: l.148/151.

trees and spaces and vegetation that had sprung up when the coppice had been felled. Life returns when the darkness is dispelled, I thought, as I stretched my weary limbs and walked over to waken Odda, my relief. He groaned and complained that he had not had long enough, as they always do, but heaved himself to his feet as I wrapped my cloak around me and found some dry leaves for a bed.

I awoke in the grey light, and went to find water. On the way back I came upon some mushrooms. I poked and kicked the fire into life again, and set them to fry in some goose fat from our supplies. The delicious aroma was enough to bring the sleepers to gather around the fire, and we broke our fast companionably, before setting back to work to finish riving our oak and hauling the timber off to the river. By the middle day we were following the horses along the ride with the last load, bearing our tools. I fell in beside Odda.

"The woodsman who keeps the horses," I said, "has been providing her food. Is there some way you can discreetly persuade him to avoid any mention to others of her departure? I will repay you when I can."

"Maybe," he replied. "It may depend upon who asked him to keep an eye on her in the beginning. I will see what I can do."

We soon emerged from the trees into the strip of land by the riverbank and unhitched the horses. Odda led them off upriver, and we set about roping up the logs and pitching them into the river, leaving the ends on the bank lest they leave without us. Gerutha sat on the bank a short way off, looking wan and anxious. I offered her some bread and cheese, but she no longer seemed hungry. She bade me sit with her.

"What will become of me, Æschere? My time approaches and I know I have no future here. If I am taken, things will go badly for me, and I do not know whether Hengest has any thought of me. I feel so alone."

I looked at her. Her sad beauty was disconcerting, so I looked away again.

"I believe Hengest thinks of you often, but to fathom his secret thought is hard, I know. I am sure that if he knew of your whereabouts he would come immediately. As for you, we will take you back to the shipwright's yard where we are staying. As I said, he knows our purpose, and his good wife, Inga, will care for your needs, I am certain. Whatever Hengest intends, from now on, I think that you will be a part of it. So be at ease, and do not worry."

"I will try," she wept, and I put my arm around her shoulder and she buried her head in mine. I think the stress of her exile was beginning to find release.

"Tell me," I said, "of your family. Are they here in Frisia?"

"Few are left now. My mother and father were drowned in a storm on their way to Frisia. I survived, and was taken in to serve the lady Hildeburh. My brother was killed in the fighting."

"I am sorry. What was his name?"

"Garulf, son of Gethwulf."

"Garulf was your brother! And you don't blame Hengest for his death?"

"We were both there, and saw what happened. My brother was a gullible fool to have listened so to Guthere's whisperings. He was courageous but rash, and I hold none other responsible for his end."

"So you are…"

"I was named for my forefather's mother, Gerutha."

"Gerutha, mother of Amleth? So you are of royal descent!"

"Yes, though not all would see it so."

Presently Odda returned, took a chunk of bread and came over to us where we sat. Through a mouthful of bread, he mumbled:

"It is well. He will not speak of the lady's absence until they ask."

"And then?"

"And then he will show them a garment that the lady left behind, besmeared and bespattered with pig's blood… and then he will tell them a story, about a wolf."

Gerutha was weeping again, but thanked Odda through her tears.

"I know not how to thank you… you have been so kind."

We unmoored our boat, and set off downriver, followed by our timber. Gerutha sat in the bow, while Heathuweald, Ralf and I rowed, and Odda stood in the stern fending off the logs with a pole when they threatened to strike or overtake us. We made rapid progress through the afternoon, rowing strongly to keep ahead of the logs until we approached the limit of the tide and the pace of the following current slackened. We soon saw the shipwright's yard, where our workmates were laying down their tools to come and watch us in, and help with the timber. Swithræd's wife and daughter had seen our approach from the house, and came down to the water's edge, full of curiosity about our extra cargo. As we touched the shore I helped Gerutha from the boat and introduced her to them, and they ushered her off to the house while I helped haul the timber to shore. We were still rolling, balancing and levering the logs into their place beneath an open-sided lean-to, where it would continue seasoning, as it got dark. Having put the timber to bed, I found my own, and slept as soundly as, well, a log.

The routine of shipyard work resumed the following morning, and the sides of the new ship started to rise. Gerutha had become as part of the shipwright's family. After two weeks I set out with Heathuweald to meet up with our comrades. We walked across marsh and field that had been submerged for much of the time since we arrived, but was now beginning to look like managed land again despite the many new meres that remained. A farmer had sown a crop of pease since the flood, in the hope of growing something to get through the winter on the newly fertile soil, although the days were already shortening, and it was as likely to end up as fodder for the beasts that had survived the floods. We weaved our way through this landscape of mud and pools, and eventually emerged on dryer land. Here and there in more sheltered places there were standing crops, but most had been beaten down by the driving rain, and would yield little. Our meeting place had been decided before we arrived in Frisia. An ancient oak tree stood on a slight rise, possibly the remains of an old terp mound. We had seen it early in the year, and its elevated position made it visible from some distance. The tree was not tall, having lost its upper branches, but broad, gnarled and fissured. We were the first there, being the closest, probably, so we sat down with our backs to the tree to wait. The day was overcast, looking like rain again, but as the morning drew towards the middle day the sky cleared again, and we saw the men walking in, one or two from each troop.

Most of us were of Hengest's original band, and we exchanged greetings and news. But Hengest was not there. The man from his troop said that he had left the morning before, bidding none to follow him or be concerned, unless he failed to return after two weeks. They had tried to persuade him not to go alone, but he had refused to take anyone with him. I told them the news of Gerutha, and they swore to pass it on as soon as they spoke to Hengest again. We agreed that someone from each troop visit the tree every week, and to leave a sign there if we needed to come together. With that we parted, and Heathuweald and I made our way back by a different path through the marshes.

Three days later, Gerutha's child arrived. I was in the yard, smoothing long boards with an adze, when I heard a woman's cries from within the house and the unmistakable squall of a baby's first complaint to the world. Gerutha had been disappointed, I know, that Hengest could not know of her whereabouts, but she would now have plenty to occupy her mind. I resumed my adzing. Tica, Swithræd's daughter, came running from the house, calling:

"Æschere! Æschere! Gerutha has a bairn! A little boy! Come, she asks for you. Come quickly!"

I laid down the adze, and walked briskly up to the house. The bairn's squalling had subsided somewhat, and I went in past the hearth to the curtained off part at the far end, where Gerutha lay drained and exhausted, but seemingly content.

"Æsc! Look! Here is a wrinkly thing. He will not keep his own counsel, not like his father!"

I took the bairn from her hands and held it up.

"Well!" I said, "here's a fine princeling!"

The bairn regarded me solemnly, and gurgled. I gave him back.

"Æsc, has there been any news?"

"None, lady. But I feel that events may begin to move. We must be patient. And you must rest. You are safe here. Be content. I will tell you as soon as I hear aught."

"I will not be content until I have seen him again. But thank you, Æsc." I nodded, and returned to my work.

The next few days saw the ship nearing completion. We worked hard from dawn until dusk, and by the end of the week we were ready to roll her from her awning down to the water's edge ready for the next tide. As the sun set, Swithræd, Heathuweald and I sat on a log near the bank, admiring our handiwork while the men started busying themselves with fitting her out. Swithræd's wife, Inga, and Gerutha came down from the house, bearing a ewer of ale and some beakers, with Tica carefully carrying the bairn. Swithræd called the rest of the men over and we all drank to the ship's good fortune.

"Have you built her for a trader?" I asked, dubiously, because her lines looked too fine for such a life.

"Nay, she is built for war. A strong keel, reinforced at the bow, plenty of oars... I have built her for Hengest. He asked me, before he left. I have seen the repairs to his ship, and what tricks he favours at sea, and made provision. I think he will be pleased."

I had not thought of how, even if we managed to recruit the men we needed, we were going to carry them all to our destination. Hengest evidently had. We lit a fire by the strand and roasted some pork, and sat together for the rest of the evening as the stars came out and a crescent moon climbed in the sky. Inga went back to the house and brought back a great bowl of barley meal and mushrooms, smelling deliciously of onions and garlic. As it grew colder, Gerutha and Tica took the bairn inside, and those who remained drew closer to the fire.

The beer was starting to make me feel drowsy, as I sat gazing into the embers and flames. Then, through the snaking air above the fire something caught my eye — a figure was picking his way through the marsh vegetation towards us. As he drew closer, I saw he was a stoutish man, cloaked and hooded, maybe slightly familiar by his gait. He entered the circle of firelight, and Swithræd stood to enquire after his business.

"I seek one who goes by the name of Æschere."

"You have found him," I said, standing also. "Eaha?"

He drew back his hood to expose his familiar features.

"Æsc! May I speak freely here?"

"Yes, they know our purpose. What is the matter? Why are you come?"

"Hengest is taken, by the king's men," he said, "they have him in fetters at the king's hall."

Silence fell as the implications churned through my mind. How had Hengest come to so careless? Odda put a beaker of ale in Eoha's hand, and some pork on a board. Eoha thanked him and went on:

"The young king has called the folk to moot in three days' time, at the King's burg, to decide his doom. We must all be there."

"How far is it from here?"

"A day's walk as the crow flies, but we should set out soon, for we may need travel more like the squirrel, to avoid being known. And we must disguise ourselves as best we can."

"Hyra's men, to the south," I said "they must be warned. Eaha, this is Swithræd, our host and master of this yard."

"Welcome, Eaha. You must be weary after your journey. Come, eat and be at ease for this night."

"Nay, my thanks, master, but as Æschere says, I must press on to fetch our comrades."

"I will go," said Heathuweald, "if I can take Ralf as guide. Swithræd, may we use your boat again?"

"Certainly."

Eoha thought for a moment. "It is well, for I am weary. But we must leave early the morning after next. If you are not back by then, you will have to follow as best you can."

"We will be coming with you also," said a voice from beyond the firelight. None had noticed that Gerutha had returned, drawn, perhaps by the urgency of the talk around the fire.

"Nay, lady, this cannot be!" I protested, "you are scarcely a week past childbirth, and we must travel speedily, and into danger."

"You will not deny me this, sir. If I am never to see him again, I will not miss this chance. You will not deny me!"

I looked at her, tall and straight, strong again, and now adamant. Swithræd intervened:

"The lady may ride if she will; my horse is gentle, and suited to carry a precious cargo."

I sighed.

"So be it."

Heathuweald and Ralf went to prepare the boat for their journey, and under the sinking moon we bade them farewell, and retired to sleep.

The morning after the next, we set out in the first light of an overcast day. With no sign of Heathuweald and Ralf, Swithræd came out to bid us farewell, and wish us the favour

111

of the goddess. As we moved across the marshes, few of us seemed to carry much hope. Eaha alone, though serious, seemed to have an air of confidence about him, although what reasons he might have had, he kept to himself. If anything, having a woman and her child made us seem more like a family band making their way to a people's gathering, than would a group of men alone. We were all lightly armed beneath our garments, with our knives; a couple of us had short swords, others a light axe, but we hoped with all our hearts that we would not need them, for we would be hideously outmatched. As we went, Gerutha and the bairn seemed to bear the journey well, the motion of the shipwright's easy old mare delighting the child when awake, and eventually lulling him to sleep. As we drew closer to the King's burg we saw more and more people converging towards it. As night fell, we made a camp at the edge of a small wood. We ate some bread with ham, cheese, and some cold pease pottage whilst the mare grazed on a nearby bank. We didn't trouble to light a fire, but wrapped ourselves in whatever we had.

I woke from a fitful sleep to a distant cockcrow. Men were on the move around me, and I helped myself to a chunk of bread from the pouch, and a mouthful of ale — it was hard to find clean water. The last few miles did not take long to cover, but the closer we drew towards the burg, the nearer we were to other folk. The new recruits had little to hide and wore their hoods back on their shoulders, but those of us who could be recognised were loath to hide ourselves too obviously. Gerutha had her head covered with a shawl, and we had our hoods drawn forward, but we felt conspicuous and a little anxious. I almost wished for rain.

The burg was raised on another great mound, much as Finnesburh had been, with a wooden palisade around the perimeter, save that part that formed the bank of a moderate river. We joined an intermittent stream of people flowing through the gates and walked up the slope, leaving our mare with some lads inside the gate who had a number of other horses in their charge already. The hall at the centre was of less stature than the great hall at Finnesburg, and on one side the ground fell away gently towards the river, free of buildings. On this ground the people were assembling, in groups of kin or district. We moved towards the top of the slope, as near the hall as we could get, and sat down on the turf to wait. I looked around the crowd, and fairly quickly picked out some of the other members of our company who were there, looking as conspicuous as we felt. For a long hour we waited as the ground filled with some hundreds of folk. Then the hall doors were opened, and two guards emerged, followed by several men of the witan and then a thirteen-year-old boy, who must have been the young king, with a more substantial armed guard of half a dozen men following him. The boy took his seat, his witan standing behind him. I wondered which of them had persuaded the king to banish Gerutha. One of the men of the witan stood forward and proclaimed in a strong voice that boomed across the field:

"People of Frisia. Your king has called you today for the purpose of determining the fate of one Octa, otherwise known as Hengest. Guards! Bring forth the captive."

A murmur rippled through the crowd as Hengest was brought out, fettered, a guard behind him holding the chain. His appearance was bedraggled, his hair plastered to his skin, his tunic torn. But he stood straight and upright. The speaker resumed:

"This man stands accused of a number of misdeeds: that he betrayed and murdered our king, Finn son of Folcwald, and despoiled his burg and took his treasure, and that he consorted with both the King's wife, Hildeburh, and her serving woman, before fleeing the land."

The young king spoke, with more assurance than I would have expected to hear from one of so few winters — a reflection, perhaps, of time spent in a Frankish court:

"My people, these events took place before my return to the land. My father ruled over you for many winters. If this man has truly committed these wrongs, then I will have vengeance for my father. I have already heard more than one account of the slaughter at Finnesburh, but I would learn more. Hengest, tell me your tale."

Hengest turned to face the king.

"My lord King," he said, "I came as a follower of Hnæf, my lord and your uncle, to stay over Yuletide, at the invitation of your father. On the night we arrived we were set upon by a number of your father's men, who besieged us in the hall. For five days we defended the hall, but on the last day your uncle and your brother who was fighting with him were slain. The long battle reached no conclusion, and an agreement was proposed whereby the feud should be set aside and referred to by none thenceforth. The survivors became, by this arrangement, your father's men. It is untrue that I consorted with your mother. My love was for Gerutha, her handmaid, and we were handfasted in the presence of the queen, your mother. She is my wife, and I would, by your leave, ask what has become of her. Of the death of your father, Finn

Folcwalding, I confess that I had a part, in that I plotted with the avenging Danes to open and hold the gates to let them in, but my true argument was with those who had stirred up an ancient and bloody feud, and caused the treacherous attack on my folk and slain my lord. I did not witness the death of your father."

"By his own mouth he admits his guilt," said the warrior who had announced the accusations. "Make an end of him now, lord king, and spare yourself any further prevarications."

"Thank you for your advice, Breossa," said the king, "but I will not act in such haste."

Now I recognised the man: we had faced him in the alleyway at Finnesburh, before he turned away to join the defence of his king at his last stand. The king continued:

"The handmaid, Gerutha. Is she not the woman you advised me to banish to a lonely place?"

"Yes, a matter in which my lord acted with wisdom."

"Did he so? Yet when your lord reflects, he wonders whether maybe he acted with more cruelty than wisdom, to send an expectant woman to such an exile. Now this man's testament sits ill with the version of events that I had already heard, at a number of points. Hengest, I would know why came you back to Frisia?'

"I came, lord King, to settle once and for all an ancient feud."

"Explain your meaning," said the king.

"As for the feud, my lord King is aware that this has touched us all. When my people were attacked by the King's Jutish warriors, I was surprised at the ferocity of the hatred that was directed against us. Since then I have endeavoured to learn more of the roots of that fierce anger, and now I think that I am able to unlock it, if the King will permit?"

"My lord King…!"

Frealaf nodded agreement, ignoring Breossa's obvious impatience, and then Hengest spoke:

"Long ago, in the time of our forefathers, the people of the Jutes raised themselves a king, a man of great craft and wisdom, Amleth by name. He ruled them with justice and was well beloved of his people. The king of the Angles, Wihtlæg, found excuse to invade the land of the Jutes and put down their king, on the grounds that the Jutes should not proclaim a king without the consent of the king of the Angles. Amleth was killed in battle by Wihtlæg, my grandfather's grandfather, and supplanted by him. This great injustice was remembered with loathing by many through the generations to this day, and resentment of the people of Angeln festered in the hearts of some of those Jutes who removed to this land. For myself, I had lived amongst Jutish men for many winters: they are doughty warriors, and most of the men that followed me were of this people, and yet, I had not reckoned on meeting such reckless hatred from among the kin of such folk. Yet meet it we did, when we came to Frisia. Since then, much blood has been spilled among my folk, and your folk, and of the Jutish men who sought shelter under your father, in the name of this feud. And that blood has fed the feud, raining new wrongs upon old. I would make an end of it, for it serves every man ill."

The king stirred, and spoke:

"And how do you propose that such an end can be achieved? Do you offer your life as redemption?"

116

"Not willingly, lord, though I am sure you may take it if you will. But such an end would not serve the purpose, but merely spread the poison further, for I too have kin who might resent such an end."

"Would you threaten me, Hengest?"

"Forgive me lord, I had not so intended, but merely wished to plainly state a consequence. But there are other reasons to spare me, if you would hear them."

"Say on."

"Part of my purpose in coming to your land was to seek help, lord. I am invited by a king of the Britons, whose name is Vortigern, to come to his land and fight his enemies. In return, he grants me land, the island named Tanatos, together with provision for my men.

"I have seen your land. It is good land, and many have come here to settle. Yet it is not secure from the sea. I have seen what the sea can do to it. The aftermath of that flood will be with you for many moons. You have not sufficient harvest to feed your people or your livestock over winter, and as I have also seen, disease already spreads. I would take some of those hungry mouths to a place without such privation, and relieve your kingdom of the burden of feeding them, making life less burdensome for those who remain. The Jutish people have come to your land to seek a better life, but their coming strains the limits of what your land can bear. Their ancient kingdom was taken from them, condemning them to live in subjection or become a wandering people. I would give them back a kingdom of their own."

With these words another murmur arose from the crowd around the field. From my position near the front I could clearly see Eaha, as could all of our men. He had made it clear to us and the other bands that no move was to be made without his prior signal, the first of two, but that all should be prepared for that signal at any point. Beside me Gerutha stood, anxious, holding the sleeping bairn wrapped in cloth.

"What say my witan to this? Ingilwulf, what say you to this man's words?" asked the king. Ingilwulf stood, a heavy man of fifty winters, and spoke:

"Lord, I know a little of the history of the Jutish people, and much of what Hengest declares is indeed so. He speaks of the perils of our current predicament, and here also I find his words ring true. I applaud his wish to end this feud, which has claimed the lives of many, not least to my lord's kin, and his aspiration to establish a new kingdom is also a laudable wish, if it can be accomplished. My lord's predicament will be to decide whether his words are to be trusted or no. For myself, having heard his words, I find little reason to mistrust what he has said."

"My thanks, Ingilwulf for your rede. Breossa, now you may have your say."

Breossa stood, and drew himself up to his full height, which was impressive. He was well built, and carried himself with easy assurance.

"My lord King. My friend Ingilwulf is easily taken in. This man, Hengest, has said much: he has shown his ability to pick up pieces of information and use them to his advantage. But all that he says is fashioned towards one end: to save his skin. I hear of his apparent desire to help my people, but even if his words are genuine, and I suspect that they are not, the Jutish people would still remain subjected to him and his Angle kin; and he seeks to take for his purposes the best of my lord's fighting men, which would leave our land further

118

weakened. I hold his wish to end this feud an impossible one. You, my lord, have suffered too many losses already. Your father sought to end the feud by agreeing a treaty of trust with this man and his allies, and was rewarded only with death for his pains, betrayed — by this same man. My friend Ingilwulf is right in one respect: my lord has to decide upon the veracity of this man's words. Nothing I have heard from this Hengest's lips this day has convinced me that he is anything but a traitor and a coward, who seeks to save himself through crafty speech and a lying tongue. His punishment should be death."

The young king considered, his eyes dropped, focussed on some point on the ground before him. The field was silent. Then he spoke.

"Thank you both for your counsel."

Then he stood, and took a step forward.

"People of Frisia, I did not call you to me this day simply to watch an entertainment. What say you? Can any of you, man or woman, vouch for this man's character?"

Immediately, a voice from near the back of the crowd called:

"Aye, lord king! I will vouch for him! But for him my family and I, and what was left of my livestock would have drowned in the floods. He braved the waters to save our lives. I vouch for him!"

Then another voice:

"And I!" I recognised the farmer we had visited in the spring.

Then more voices, some saying:

"Nay! He betrayed our king! Kill the traitor!" and others, some of them voices I recognised as being our young recruits, piped up, until it was impossible to hear what individuals were saying. The boy king raised his hand:

"Thank you, my people, thank you. Hengest, I find that you have divided my people in their thoughts on your doom. My ruling is therefore this. Breossa! You may have your chance to avenge my father —" in an instant, Breossa's sword left its sheath, and beside me, Eaha's walking staff raised to his right shoulder. There was a movement in the crowd, hardly perceptible as everyone drew further towards the front: a defensive ring was invisibly forming within the front of the crowd. The king continued:

"Hold fast there, Breossa, and allow me finish! Kerb your eagerness. I would not have any man killed in cold blood. We will put this to the trial. Send for the smith, and have those chains struck off. Clear the ground before me. They will need room to move. Breossa, you claim that this man is a traitor and a coward. That remains to be seen. Guards, furnish this man with a weapon and a shield."

As Breossa's sword lowered, and he took a step backward, looking crestfallen, Eaha's staff slowly returned to rest. The crowd was abuzz as they waited while the smith brought his tools. Hengest was offered various weapons, choosing an ashen spear to go with his shield, while the crowd was shepherded back a dozen paces by the guards. The two men walked into the space before the king, and turned to face one another. Breossa had picked up a shield, and was wearing a jerkin of mail-rings which might resist a slash from a sword, but were too wide to resist a spear thrust. Hengest wore nought but his ripped tunic.

"Let the trial begin, and the doom decided," declared the king. By my left side, Gerutha grabbed my arm. She was as

tense as a bowstring. The babe slept on. I squeezed her hand
to calm her. Eoha shifted his staff to the other hand, but it
remained touching the ground.

The two men circled one another, each seeking an
opening; Breossa's sword was active, swinging down to find
a gap in his opponent's guard. Each time it was parried by
Hengest's shield, and a counter thrust from the spear would
test Breossa's agility.

"We have faced one another before," muttered Breossa,
between blows.

"Aye," Hengest replied, "how did you come to escape
from your King's last defence?"

"Beaten senseless. Came to before they came for the dead,
and left when I saw how things were." He flicked his head
sideways to avoid a jab from Hengest's spear.

"You know this king has finished with you?" Hengest
murmured. From my place at the front of the crowd I could
just about hear their breathless voices. The king was too far
away.

"Ha! You think so?"

"Why else would he throw you in the path of the
Stallion?"

"You flatter yourself..."

"Come with me to Britain."

"Nay, I think not... this boy king needs me yet... to
defend him from... men such as you."

"Gerutha... what have you done with her...?"

"Ah... naughty girl... banished to a grove in the woods..."

"Is that how you treat your own?"

"Lucky not to be hanged... for a traitor. Shame... a fair
wench she was..."

"Was…?"

"Hm… now lies in the belly of a wolf, I hear."

Hengest's shoulders stiffened and his face changed, his look turning grim and dangerous. He launched a mighty spear thrust at Breossa's chest, but the man was ready for it, and interposed his shield just in time as the point lodged deep in the lime wood and stuck. In an instant Breossa's sword swung down, severing the spear shaft near the head. Eaha's arm twitched a little, but then resumed its stillness. Breossa was advancing, his sword blows gradually carving great chunks from Hengest's shield, but a furious lunge from the metal boss of that same shield knocked him back a step, and then Hengest was down on one knee and the decapitated spear shaft was swinging in a great backhanded hissing arc. It smashed into Breossa's inner knee, forcing a stifled scream from the man, as he stumbled backwards further, and then Hengest was on him, battering him to the ground with the shield boss. Casting the shield aside and quartering the staff, Hengest brought it down on Breossa's wrist and the sword spun off to the side. The jagged end of the wooden shaft came to rest against the prone man's gorget, and silence fell. Hengest's jaw tightened as he tensed to avenge his wife.

"Hengest!"

A woman's voice, cutting through the silence. I looked round, and there was Gerutha, now bareheaded, the great flag of her bright hair shining in the sunlight, calling to her loved one; and the bairn, awoken by the cry, started to squall. All heads turned. Hengest blinked, as if awakening from a strange dream. When the recumbent Breossa turned his head back from the sight of the woman, he no longer looked up a length of wooden shaft, but at an extended hand.

"Come with me!" said Hengest.

And Breossa grasped the hand, and the dread chain was broken.

The two men turned to face the king, and bowed. The young man beckoned them forward.

"Hengest, I will now pronounce my doom, which is this: with this, the feud will end. As my father intended, so do I, that none should speak of it or call it to mind. You are free to leave, with such warriors as will follow you, to seek the shores of Britain. How many do you intend to take?"

"A hundred, lord King. But I will presently need more: farmers to tend the land and stock, woodsmen, builders, as well as warriors and families. I will send ships for more."

"See that you do, for that young woman and the child will remain here as surety of your word, until the next sending. I regret having treated her unkindly, and ask your forgiveness for that. Breossa! What think you? Will you go with Hengest and set behind you your counsels of hatred?"

"I will, lord King, and I ask for your pardon."

"And I grant it most willingly."

"Now, before you go and greet your wife and child, Hengest, I would detain you for a few moments longer. I would know from you the tale of my brother's death."

"Yes, my lord King."

They walked back into the hall in earnest conversation.

A short while later, they emerged, and Hengest walked, then ran, down to where a group of us stood in the crowd, and into the arms of Gerutha. The child squawked, and Hengest took him and held him up delightedly. He turned to the crowd.

"People of Frisia! I ask your forgiveness for the wrongs of the past. But I will make a new kingdom for those who will follow me. And to rule that kingdom, I will give you a king! Behold Oisc, scion of the great king Amleth of old."

He held the boy aloft, to a great cheer from the crowd.

"Oisc, Hengest?" asked Gerutha.

"Yes… what's wrong with Oisc?"

"It is an odd name, and sounds strange."

"Well, it's too late now. Maybe if we say it quickly it will sound like Æsc, here?"

She thumped his chest.

"Idiot!" she said.

On a crisp morning before winter, we rowed out of our estuary, whilst watching our new ship across the water as she hoisted her sail for the first time. We had bidden Swithræd and his folk farewell on the staithe. Hengest and Gerutha had parted with much sorrow, and he now sat with us, thoughtfully watching the operation across the water. Happily, Ralf and Odda had been released by Swithræd to come with us, for we would need their skills in days to come, and now we watched as they directed men to haul this rope or that. The wind was blowing south-westerly, and once we cleared the islands it would be before us, but here it was gentle and soon filled the great sail, wafting the ship northward. We fell in astern of it, easily keeping pace until the waters opened into the great mere and we managed to overtake her. Between the two ships, we now had full crews of fighting men, Jutes and Frisians, as well as some of their families and a few pigs and sheep. As the mere opened further, we saw a familiar sail in the distance. Hengest had sent for Horsa in the days since the trial at King's burg. I saw Swæfi, and not a few Angle warriors amongst their crew. As the ships drew within hailing distance, Hengest called:

"Hey! Horsa! Your arse will grow fat, now you don't have to row any more!"

"From what I've been hearing, it'll never grow as fat as your head, brother!" came the riposte amidst ribald laughter.

Now we had to turn into the wind, and the sails struck down from the other ships. Their sweeps emerged and we turned west to thread the gap between the first island and the main, before turning directly into the breeze to follow the coast down. The sea was choppy, and some of us were soon busy bailing again, but as the day went on, the wind died down. We passed the mouths of the Rhine river before the following dawn, having kept going through the night in watches, now pulling steadily through a gentle swell. During the following night we struck out from the coast into the open sea. At first light we caught our first view of the cliffs of the land of the Britons on the horizon. They grew steadily closer, and as the sun arose, I was awestruck by their pure white beauty. Over them, ravens circled in great, majestic arcs. Behind them was a land of grassy down and woodland wonderfully decked out in red and golden hues, sloping down to a sand and shingle spit at the end of a long bay. Over the ground to the south of the spit we could just see a fortified stone burh, immensely strong, rising over the marshes. Along a ridge above the beach, a small troop of horsemen rode towards the place where we would land. Hengest set our ship for the shore, and the others followed us in. We felt the first touch, and then the ships were grating up the shingle, and men were leaping over the side to secure them.

We had arrived in the land of the Britons.

*

From *The Husband's Message*

He who engraved this wood bade me ask thee
that thou, treasure-adorned, shouldst call to thy mind
the promises which you two often spoke in earlier days,
while yet you might have your abode in the mead-halls,
live in the same land, enjoy friendship.

Feud drove him away from the victorious people;
now he himself has bidden me tell thee joyfully,
that thou shouldst cross the sea, when on the edge of the cliffs
thou hast heard the sad cuckoo cry in the grove.

After that let no living man hold thee from the journey
or hinder thy going. Go seek the sea, the home of the gull!
Board the ship, so that south from here
thou mayest find thy husband over the path of the sea,
where thy lord lives in hopes of thee.

Nor may a wish in the world come more to his mind,
from what he said to me, than that you two should be granted
that together you may afterwards give treasure,
studded armlets, to warriors and companions.

He has enough treasures of beaten gold,
though in a foreign land he holds his dwelling,
in a fair country. Many proud heroes wait upon him,
though here my friendly lord, driven by necessity,
launched his boat and was forced
to go forth alone on the stretch of the waves,
on the way of the flood, to furrow the ocean streams,
eager for departure.

Now the man has overcome woe;
he lacks not his desires, nor horses, nor treasures,
nor mead-joys, none of the precious stores of earls on the
earth, O prince's daughter, if he may only enjoy thee,
in spite of the old threat against you two.

I join F, R, EA, W and D to assure thee
that as long as he lives, he will love you,
faithful to the vows you two
spoke to one another long ago.

Historical Notes:

1] Sources:

Having delivered Hengest to the shores of Kent, I can now claim that the rest is history! Or maybe legend, or at least tradition. His subsequent rebellion against his British masters, and the conquest of Kent, are recorded in the annals of the *Anglo-Saxon Chronicle* [x], Bede's *History of the English Church and People (Historia Ecclesiastica)*[xi], the *History of Britain (Historia Brittonum)* of Nennius[xii], and Gildas' *On the ruin of Britain (De Excidio Britanniae)*[xiii].

Gildas was a British (Welsh) monk, writing some seventy years after the events, and forty years after the decisive British victory at Badon Hill, probably from a monastery in the north-west of Britain. His knowledge of events in the south-east of Britain was limited, and his theme was to identify what had happened to his country as divine retribution for sins past and present, as a corrective to his readers, particularly those who ruled in his time, and this limits the historical usefulness of his testimony. As his account is the closest we have to a contemporary record, however, we cannot ignore it; indeed, the venerable Bede, our exemplary eighth century English historian follows him closely in many areas. The kingdom of Kent was to last for 300 years, strangely agreeing with the report of the soothsayer in Gildas. Its first king, and the man who was to give his name to its royal line, was not Hengest the war-leader, but Oisc, his son.

The *Anglo-Saxon Chronicle*, on the other hand, follows Bede in its statement of the origins of the Germanic settlers of Britain. It lists the battles of Hengest and Æsc (Oisc), forbearing to mention the victor, but often commenting in terms of outcome in language which is sometimes reminiscent of heroic verse (for example: '… and the Welsh fled from the English as from fire'). It also contains archaic place-names which may have come from another early source. It was begun in Wessex during the time of Alfred the Great, whose mother, the king's biographer Asser[xiv] informs us, was a Jute.

Saxo Grammaticus, a Dane writing in the twelfth century, collected all he could find of the history of the country he then knew as Denmark in his *Danish History*[xv]. When reading his work it is as well to bear in mind that there was a tendency for tribes other than the Danes to be absorbed into Danish history as Danish themselves. An example of this occurs at the outset of his work he states that there were two forefathers of the nation, Dan and Angul, but thenceforth the name 'Angul' seems to disappear. In the extract from *Widsith*, King Offa (here listed as a ruler of the Angles) makes a new boundary on the Eider. Saxo gives an account of this fight, in which he lists Offa (Uffo) as a Dane, and his enemy the Saxons, who he claims lost, with their defeat, control of their own land. It seems to me to be possible that the prize Offa (of Angeln) won was rather the land of the Swæfe, a northern branch of the Swabian folk based around Schwabsted, which passed from the control of the Saxons (or Myrgings?) to that of the Angles, providing that people with a useful conduit to the North Sea.

The author known as Nennius writes from a Welsh perspective, and has selected from a gathered 'heap' of sources the material for his account. His account of the migration is at variance with that of the *Anglo-Saxon Chronicle* at a number of points, and paints Hengest as an unscrupulous and devious man, 'in whom united craft and penetration'. The veracity of the story of 'the Night of the Long Knives', wherein Hengest plans the murder of 300 British nobles under the flag of truce, I would leave the reader to judge for themselves. Similarly challenging is the story of Hengest's daughter and her part in the British cessation of Kent. Alan Bliss reckons that Hengest's age at the time of the *Freswæl* must have been twenty-five or thirty at most: this places some doubt on Nennius' claims that Hengest had grown sons and an adult daughter (with whom King Vortigern supposedly becomes infatuated, an obsession that leads him to cede the whole kingdom of Kent to the then supposedly defeated 'Saxons').

2] Names:

It may be possible with regard to the 'sons' of Hengest that Nennius has drawn two different accounts of the same event from his heap and treated them as separate events in time, mistakenly creating a loop in his account; and that the true names of Hengest and Horsa, as Bliss suggests, were Octa and Ebissa[xvi]. Whether or not this is so, I have used these names in my tale.

Alan Bliss, in his appendix to *Finn and Hengest*,[xvii] draws a comparison between the king lists of Kent and Mercia, and I have found this most useful in my attempt to calculate a time frame for this story, so I will repeat it here, slightly modified:

Estimated birth dates	Mercia	Kent
	Woden	Woden
300	Wihtlæg	
330	Wermund	Wehta
360	Offa	Witta (appt. ruler of Swæfe?)
390	Angeltheow	Wihtgils
420	Eomær	Hengest
450	Icel	Oisc

Bliss notes the occurrence of 'Wiht' names in both genealogies, strongly suggesting a common parent: here suggested that Wehta was a brother of Wermund, both being sons of Wihtlæg.

Most of the names of characters not already mentioned in the literature are taken, for want of 'Jutish' names, from the Kentish dens; K. P. Witney suggests that some of these names may well belong to the companions who first landed with Hengest[xviii]. The chapter names are taken or compounded from Klaeber's glossary[xix] and the glossary in the *Cambridge Old English Reader*.

3] Translations of heroic verse:

The translations from *The Finnesburh Fragment, Beowulf, The Wife's Lament, Maxims II* and *The Husband's Message* are my adaptations of versions to be found in Tolkien (1982), *Anglo-Saxon Poetry* (R K Gordon), *Anglo-Saxon Poetry* (S A J Bradley, 1995), and *The Cambridge Old English Reader* (R Marsden 2015). The extract from *Widsith* is from Chambers (2012[1912]).

4] Archaeology:

The sea-lane used so much in my tale between the shores of Jutland and the meres of the Netherlands, bounded by the Frisian Islands, might be seen as analogous with the motorways of today. J. N. L. Myers traces finds of Jutish pottery all the way down this route and into Kent and beyond[xx]. Although a hazardous mode of transport, travel by ship was probably a great deal more secure than overland routes through hostile tribal lands.

Conclusion:

This story has been about the people who were to become the *Cantware,* the people of Kent. I leave you with K. P. Witney's summary of the legacy of Hengest's career from his book *The Kingdom of Kent:*[xxi]

'[When] Oisc's rule had become firmly established, the people were left in the enjoyment of the rich prize which Hengest had won for them. It is true that his appearance in Kent was no more than a continuation of a long period of mercenary employment, settlement and infiltration, but this does not in any way diminish his achievement. The conquest of Kent was different from anything that had gone before; a systematic occupation of territory, from which there emerged the first of the English kingdoms, a society knit by common obligations of loyalty and observing a common custom. The triumph of the Jutes was bound to act as an example to others, and the effect of their victories in destroying the defences of the British around London exposed the whole of the south to the gathering strength of the invaders. It remains difficult to deny that Hengest's coming marks the one sure beginning of the English nation.'

i] J. R. R. Tolkien, ed. Alan Bliss, *Finn and Hengest, the Fragment and the Episode.* George Allen & Unwin 1982.

ii] Bede, trans. L. Sherley-Price *A History of the English Church and People (Historia Ecclesiastica),* Harmondsworth, Penguin. (Penguin Classics)1968.

iii] Adapted from translations in: J. R. R. Tolkien, ed. Alan Bliss, *Finn and Hengest, the Fragment and the Episode.* George Allen & Unwin 1982; Richard Marsden, *The Cambridge Old English Reader,* Cambridge University Press, 2015.

iv] Adapted from translations in: J. R. R. Tolkien, ed. Alan Bliss, *Finn and Hengest, the Fragment and the Episode.* George Allen & Unwin 1982; Richard Marsden, *The Cambridge Old English Reader,* Cambridge University Press, 2015.

v] J. R. R. Tolkien, ed. Alan Bliss, *Finn and Hengest, the Fragment and the Episode.* George Allen & Unwin 1982.

vi] R. W. Chambers. *Widsith, A Study in Old English Heroic Legend,* Forgotten Books, 2012.

vii] Adapted from translations in: *Anglo-Saxon Poetry,* R. K. Gordon, London, J. M. Dent & Sons (Everyman); *Anglo-Saxon Poetry,* S. A. J. Bradbury, London, J. M. Dent & Sons (Everyman) 1995; Richard Marsden, *The Cambridge Old English Reader,* Cambridge University Press, 2015.

viii] Adapted from translations in: *Anglo-Saxon Poetry,* R. K. Gordon, London, J. M. Dent & Sons (Everyman); *Anglo-Saxon Poetry,* S. A. J. Bradbury, London, J. M. Dent & Sons (Everyman) 1995.

ix] J. R. R. Tolkien, ed. Alan Bliss, *Finn and Hengest, the Fragment and the Episode.* 1982, George Allen & Unwin 1982. [pp63-76]

x] Trans. G. N. Garmonsway, *The Anglo-Saxon Chronicle*, London, J. M. Dent & Sons, (Everyman) 1953.

xi] Bede, Trans. L. Sherley-Price, *History of the English Church and People (Historia Ecclesiastica)*, 1968, Harmondsworth, Penguin. Penguin Classics.

xii] Nennius, trans. J. A. Giles: *History of the Britons (Historia Brittonum)* Milton Keynes, Lightning Source UK.

xiii] Gildas, trans. J. A. Giles: *On the Ruin of Britain (De Excidio Britanniae)*, Rockville (Maryland), Serenity, 2009.

xiv] Asser, trans. Simon Keynes and Michael Lapidge, *Alfred the Great*, London, Penguin Books (Penguin Classics) 1983.

xv] Saxo Grammaticus, trans. O. Elton, *The Danish History of Saxo Grammaticus,* Forgotten Books, 2008.

xvi] J. R. R. Tolkien, ed. Alan Bliss, *Finn and Hengest, the Fragment and the Episode.* George Allen & Unwin 1982.

xvii] J. R. R. Tolkien ed. Alan Bliss, *Finn and Hengest, the Fragment and the Episode.* George Allen & Unwin 1982.

xviii] K. P. Witney, *The Kingdom of Kent,* London & Chichester, Phillimore, 1982.

xix] F. Klaeber, *Beowulf and The Fight at Finnsburg,* Boston, D. C. Heath & Co. 1950.

xx] J. N. L. Myers, *The English Settlements,* Oxford, OUP 1986.

xxi] K. P. Witney, *The Kingdom of Kent,* London & Chichester, Phillimore, 1982.